The Table

Matthew Waynee

Galt Art House
Los Angeles
www.galtarthouse.com

Third Printing

ISBN: 1-931170-26-6 (pbk.)

Printed in the United States of America
Cover photograph permission from Paul Peloquin

To
Al & Rita

Table of Contents

The Table

Book One
of
The Bay City Trilogy

Matt Wayne
July 5th, 2002

Part One

1

October 1918

The foreman yelled the name Stash Janowicz three times before Andrzej Kowalczyk turned and answered.

"What's the matter with you, Janowicz?" his boss snapped, "You going deaf?"

"No, sir," Kowalczyk muttered, "I was thinking."

"I'm not paying you to think. Keep picking."

Kowalczyk grumbled under his breath and bent back over the dusty row of onions. He dug a ripe bulb from the dirt and tossed it into the burlap sack beside him. This was how the field hands spent their shifts, crouched under the blazing Texas sun. The furnace blasts of wind offered little relief and sucked the moisture from their throats. By the end of the day, the harvesters were indistinguishable from their sacks—sweaty, grimy, and frayed. Only the booze and gambling at Tavo's gave them any solace.

The foreman made it clear how worthless the workers were. The crops were important, shipped to Europe for the soldiers fighting in the Great War. Those men were heroes, defending their country and honoring their families. The field hands were a disgrace. Nearly every one of them had found a way to avoid military service, preferring to spend their days on their hands and knees picking crops for others.

But for Andrzej Kowalczyk, fighting in Europe was what he dreamed about. The camaraderie among soldiers. The glory of freeing French villages from the Kaiser's troops. That was where he wanted to be. Working in the fields was only temporary. He just needed to find a way out of his obligation.

His boss stood in the distance, barking orders at two field hands. Kowalczyk gathered his courage, scrambled to his feet, and trudged toward him.

"Sir. Sir. I need a favor."

"Wait till tomorrow," the foreman called over his shoulder.

"It can not wait." Kowalczyk grabbed his arm.

The foreman spun around. "Don't ever touch me again, Janowicz."

Kowalczyk snatched his hand back and dared to raise his cowering, forty-four-year-old body to match his boss' powerful build. "I need an advance on next week's pay."

The foreman laughed in his face. "I just paid you three days ago."

"Please, I need the money."

"I warned you about Tavo's dice."

"I do not gamble," Kowalczyk protested.

"Don't lie to me, Janowicz. I hear you're in deep."

"It is for my family. Back home."

"Family? You told me you didn't have one."

Kowalczyk looked down. "I have a wife in Michigan. But no children."

The foreman grunted in disbelief. "What's to stop you from running back to her with my money?"

"I need this work."

"Then get back to it." His boss shooed him away.

Kowalczyk stood his ground. "You can pay me each day. After I finish my shift."

"If I do that for you, I'll have to do that for everyone."

Kowalczyk lowered his voice. "I will give you ten percent."

The foreman scoffed and turned away.

"Twenty," Kowalczyk pleaded.

His boss paused.

"Yes," Kowalczyk scurried closer, "twenty percent. All for you."

"You need the money, huh?"

He nodded.

"All right, I'll help you," the foreman said with a grin, "for fifty."

"Half my pay?" Kowalczyk gasped, "I can not afford that."

"Then I guess you don't need the money."

"I do."

"That's what it'll cost you. You don't like it, wait till next Friday."

"But—"

"Now get back to work, Janowicz, before I dock you half a day's pay."

Kowalczyk raised his hands to protest but said nothing. He swore to himself and stomped back up the row to his burlap sack.

2

As the buzz of the electric saw howled from inside the barn beside her, Tekla Kowalczyk lifted an axe high above her head. She was a thin, thirty-year-old woman whose wiry frame unleashed such resilience and power that the blade tore through the log in one swipe. She tossed the split pieces to the side and set a fresh log on the cutting stump. Tekla had already cut enough firewood to last through even the harshest Michigan winter, but she tried to keep her mind from returning to the war. However that was impossible to do with her days spent at Wilson's sewing fabric for the wings of DH-4 bombers and her nights at home with her two boys, Ty and Stanley.

Unlike most of the Polish immigrant families in the South End of Bay City, the Kowalczyks were fortunate to own their own land. Their barn stood at the back of the lot where the saw still whirled away inside, biting through plank after plank. Fifty yards to the front was the three bedroom house that had been built decades earlier before the lumber boom died. Over 70,000 people had assumed the timber would last forever. Now, it was all but gone. The shanty boys with their saws and axes had devoured most of the forest in a generation's time, destroying the very thing Bay City needed to survive. Leeches, Tekla thought, feeding on those around them. Like so many she knew.

She set another log on the stump and didn't notice old man Toporski scooting up the front yard with his mail sack.

"Good day, Tekla," he grumbled, his voice gruff from decades of tobacco. "How are you?"

She looked up with a tired smile. "Keeping busy, Dziadzia. How are you?"

"The sun rises the same every day."

"How's Busia?" she asked, pulling her auburn hair out of her face.

"Canning the last of the vegetables. I'll bring you some sweet pickles and beets when she's done."

"Good." Tekla set the axe down and leaned against the barn wall. "Anything from Andrzej?"

Toporski shook his bald head and handed her a few pieces of mail. "Sorry."

"It's been over two months."

"Don't worry yourself," he assured her. "The army has to keep his mission secret."

"I know, but a postcard. Anything."

"Remember, no news is good news."

"I just wonder where he is."

"When he returns, he'll be proud of what you've done here," Dziadzia offered, trying to change the subject.

"We'll see."

"You should hear what they say around town," Toporski added. "Jarik Wolczyk delivers on Center Avenue and tells all of his houses about Ty's tables."

"Really?"

"That boy's the hardest worker I know."

"That boy worries me. He works all day and barely sleeps at night." She pointed to an untouched plate of cabbage pierogis on a stool beside the barn door. "His lunch has been there for hours. He'll go half the day, sometimes all day without eating. When I ask, he says he forgot. How do you forget to eat?"

"Young boys are machines, Tekla."

"He's going to hurt himself one of these days."

"Don't worry yourself. Ty's a good boy."

Dziadzia was trying to be optimistic, so she nodded. "Any news around the South End?"

Toporski shrugged. "The Sinickis on 24th."

Tekla shook her head.

"They live next to the Ciszeks, across from the Jakubczaks. Their boy's being shipped home."

"What happened?"

"His parents don't know. The army only said he's coming home."

"I'll be glad when this war's over." Tekla paused. In the distance, Franek Kowalczyk, Andrzej's older brother, was walking up the path.

Toporski's eyes followed her glare. "I should finish my route," he said. "Tell the boys I said hello."

"I will."

Dziadzia said goodbye and walked away, greeting Franek as he passed.

Tekla snatched the axe, turned her back to her brother-in-law, and drove the blade through the standing log.

3

Almost a century before in the early 1800s, white settlers first arrived along the shores of Lake Huron in central Michigan where the Saginaw River flowed through the vast stretches of virgin pines. These rugged men purchased tracts of land from the Ojibwa tribe and fought against the surrounding swamps and mosquitoes for space to build their first homes. Frontiersmen from Ohio, Pennsylvania, and Virginia trickled into the area and sent word of the endless trees back to their families and friends. By 1840, waves of settlers surged to mid-Michigan, and within a decade's time, a city on the lake was forged, complete with a dozen operating sawmills that ignited Bay City's lumber boom.

Orders for timber flooded in from around the country. Local mill owners enticed shanty boys into their crews and paid them handsomely. In a flurry of saws and axes and chains, these lumberjacks attacked the woods and endured the frigid winds and constant snowfall. The shanty boys struggled to keep warm with their full, mangled beards and thick layers of wool as frost gnawed their flesh. Sometimes, a man was found at day break, frozen in his sleep.

The rest continued on.

They huddled around breakfast fires and rubbed the aches and chill from their stiff bodies. All day long towering trees crashed to the ground and shook the earth. Trunks were hauled across icy trails and stacked along the riverbanks. Careless shanty boys were crushed under falling trees, and even the most experienced men could be smashed beneath an avalanche of logs that snapped free from a chained stack. New lumberjacks were continually sent to the camps to replace the exhausted and the maimed. They prayed they wouldn't suffer the same fate.

When spring arrived, the ice and snow melted and filled the riverbeds, and the stored logs were dumped into the flowing waters. Expert river hogs navigated the trees downstream. The glut of timber kept these men running in their spiked boots from log to log, yanking jammed trunks free. Throughout the season, many lost their footing and splashed into the river. The fortunate ones only had to withstand the bruises and insults from fellow hogs as they pulled themselves out of the water unharmed. Others had their heads crushed between colliding logs or became trapped under the ceiling of trunks and drowned.

By the beginning of summer, the trees reached the mouth of the Saginaw River and were corralled into more than sixty lumberyards and sawmills. The shanty boys abandoned their axes and warm clothes and found jobs inside these hot boxes. Fourteen hours a day of sweltering heat and dusty air. Workers coughed up sawdust all evening long, only to return to the suffocating mills the next morning. Water-driven circular saws were slow and took fifteen minutes to rip a board, offering more chances for blades to chomp off fingers and hands. Worse still, blades sometimes shattered mid-log and shot metal fragments through the air that tore into the heads and chests of workers.

When faster, more efficient saws were developed, blades buzzed through lumber in record time. Mill owners couldn't find enough men to keep pace, so they offered lofty wages to lure more workers to the area. Countless immigrants from Canada, France, Germany, and Poland poured in. It was with the immigrant surge of 1875 that Franek Kowalczyk arrived in the Polish South End of Bay City with his two brothers and their father Vladimir.

As a teenager, Franek refused to work and was at constant battle with his father, who tried to reestablish the family woodworking business in America. Picking up supplies, sawing lumber, sanding pieces, delivering products were all beneath Franek. This struggle continued until 1898 when he and his older brother Tomaszius joined the local 33rd Regiment and shipped out to Cuba to fight in the Spanish-American War, leaving Andrzej behind to help with the business.

Franek returned to Bay City alone the following year and was honored as the only Polish hero from the campaign. With his new popularity, he started his own store and bought merchandise from other craftsmen around the Polish neighborhood. Vladmir was outraged by this insult and demanded an apology. But Franek remained indifferent to him, and Andrzej received the brunt of their father's wrath.

Customers packed into Franek's store and listened to his heroic tales of the Battle of Santiago and purchased everything they needed for their homes. Rugs, pots, tools, chairs, leather. Profits soared, and Franek amassed a small fortune. When the lumber industry in Bay City bottomed out in 1905, it became impossible for local craftsmen to make any money, so they sold their products to Franek below cost. With his oily smile and slippery words, he resold their fine pieces to the wealthy citizens living along Center Avenue. The craftsmen in the South End were infuriated with Franek's interactions with the upper class. Unless cheap labor for menial jobs was needed, those wealthy citizens had nothing to do with the Polish community.

But Franek thought they were all overreacting. A

business deal was a business deal. To calm their anger, Franek offered loans of all sizes to families in the South End and often extended their due dates when payments were difficult. Many Polish families were in great debt to Franek. This secured him a respected and influential place in the South End circle. He was especially popular at Pulaski Hall, a local speakeasy where the older men could sneak a drink of homemade liquor during the state-wide prohibition of the Great War. There, they played cards and complained about the German, French-Canadian, and Irish workers who stole jobs from them at the new shipyard. Franek's stories of guarding Spanish prisoners or fighting at Santiago made their economic strains a little easier to forget.

Recently, though, something new consumed their drinking hours. One of their Pulaski brothers was in Europe making history. The men had all heard how on the night before the local 33rd shipped out of Texas, Andrzej Kowalczyk had been pulled from training. Several boys had written home to their families explaining how Mr. Kowalczyk had been reassigned to a secret battalion. Pulaski Hall roared with excitement as the men argued whether Andrzej was a member of General Pershing's Expeditionary Force or part of the great defensive stand against the Germans at Marne. As every debated mission escalated, glasses of vodka were raised to Andrzej Kowalczyk, the South End's greatest military hero.

Franek did his best to force down his drink and smile. But sometimes it was too much. As it was on this evening. Franek excused himself from the group, grabbed his hat, and left the Hall as a new legend about his brother materialized behind him.

It was on his walk back to the store when he decided to stop by Andrzej's home.

"Hello Tekla," Franek called from the clearing.

She tore the axe through another hunk of log.

"How are the boys?"

"Fine."

"Have you heard from Andrzej?"

"No."

Franek stared as Tekla continued to chop. "What do you want, Franek?" she said without looking up.

"Christ, Tekla," he objected with his smile, "can't I visit my family?"

"You can. But you never do, unless you need to talk about the shop."

"That's not fair."

"So there's nothing about your business?"

"No. I was just wondering about Andrzej."

"As I said, I haven't heard anything. Goodbye, Franek."

She set another log on the stump.

Franek turned away, then stopped. "Tekla, there is one thing."

She ripped the axe through the wood. "I knew it."

"You're making a big mistake going door to door. You should be here working."

She glared at him.

"I'm trying to help," he stammered.

"Help? You didn't pay us enough to—"

"Hear me out, Tekla. If you sell me your tables again, I'll pay you six dollars more for each one."

"Six dollars? We make more than that on our own."

"I need those tables. People keep asking for them. You know how I look when my own family won't sell to me? You should hear them talk at Pulaski's."

"I don't care what they say."

"They talk about Andrzej and his business," he stressed. "He won't like that."

"He isn't here to not like it, Franek." She checked her anger. "If you want our tables, pay us what we ask."

"I can't make a profit at that price."

"That's not my concern."

"You owe me. I've always taken care of you. Back when Andrzej struggled."

"Everybody struggled then."

"But I still bought his tables, and I paid him more than those pieces were worth."

"Andrzej's work was never that bad, and you know it."

The barn door slid open, and a voice called out, "Uncle Stash!" A lanky boy of fifteen raced into the twilight, wiping sawdust from his face. He stopped.

"How are you, Ty?" Franek reached out his hand. "I haven't seen you in a while."

Ty cleared his throat and spit. "What does he want, mother?"

Franek laughed off the comment. "Ty, we're just talking about your father."

"Your uncle is leaving."

"But Tekla—"

"Goodbye, Franek."

He wrung his hands together. "Yes, I should return to the store. Ty, we'll talk tomorrow."

His nephew stared with his arms folded across his chest as Franek walked away.

4

A loaded satchel of newspapers bounced off Stanley's back as he sprinted to his favorite stop along his paper route. The eleven-year-old climbed onto the bottom rung of the wooden fence and gazed across the open field. Lionel DeRemer and Henry Dora tinkered on a bi-winged machine. These men were famous as far as Stanley was concerned. They had attended flight school in New York and had flown with the Wright Brothers. Now, they finished the last check of their own flyer.

But their machine didn't compare to the mighty vehicles his father flew over France. His DH-4 soaring high above wounded soldiers. His Sopwith Camel shooting down enemy birds. Stanley played out his father's exploits on his typewriter, pecking away one finger at a time. Fokker triplanes. Lewis machine guns. American flying aces. Castor oil and petrol fuel. Facts and imaginations woven together in stories about his father's secret mission. Stanley got most of his details from Miss Noonan, his grade school teacher. She shared articles and photographs with the class. The best information came from the letters she read from her fiancé who served in Europe. He was a pilot just like Stanley's father.

But his father hadn't sent him a single letter from his mission so Stanley signed up to work as a delivery boy to learn as much as he could. How else could a boy be the first to clip out the latest reports from the warfront? Every morning at five forty-five, Stanley raced to the *Times-Tribune* office and picked up his bundle. On his dash to school, he'd flip through the pages, searching for any interesting tidbits to give to Miss Noonan. She'd thank him with her endearing smile, and Stanley would get flustered, unable to hide his blush. Everyday, he stayed after school and talked to Miss Noonan about his latest stories or news from Europe or her fiancé's letters. One day, Stanley told her he wanted to be a newspaper reporter when he grew up and write real stories without using any imagined details. Miss Noonan told him that it was sometimes impossible to separate imagination from the truth. Stanley didn't believe this, so she explained to him how not everything in the newspaper was completely accurate. Some stories were posted days, weeks, or months after the events happened. And often the reporters who wrote the stories weren't even there, so details could become distorted after being passed from one person to the next until finally reaching the journalist. Stanley doubted this. She said she could prove it.

The next day Miss Noonan had the class play a game. She whispered a sentence from the newspaper to Cecil Gaffke who passed it to Ruth Sampson who repeated it up the first row and back down the second, until Stanley heard from Reginald Towey that American troops captured German spies sneaking up on their army command post near St. Mihiel, which he told to Harriet Mueller who spread it on to the other nineteen students until Julius Padget stood up and recited to the class what Mitzy Clemens told him: German spies commanded American troops into the battle at St. Michael.

Stanley's jaw dropped open.

Then Miss Noonan read the original sentence out loud: German troops suspected American spies had infiltrated their army command near St. Mihiel. Stanley couldn't believe his ears. Even the best newspaper reporters were mixing facts with imagination. His eyes beamed with pride. He was already writing like a real reporter.

The sputtering chug of the engine brought Stanley's attention back to the field. Dora cranked the engine again as DeRemer gave the propeller a whirl. The motor revved to life. DeRemer climbed into the driver seat while his partner backed away from the machine. The airplane lurched forward, inching around, until its nose pointed down the runway. Then the winged machine accelerated up the path and struggled to lift itself off the ground, wobbling and skipping as it fought the force of gravity. Five feet, ten feet, twenty, until it was finally in the air.

Stanley knew one day he would fly above the South End and yell down to his family. They would wave back, envious of his adventure, but be too frightened to soar as high. Everyone, that is, except for his father, who would cherish what it was like to fly.

5

During the height of the lumber boom in the late 1800s, there was one week between the winter cutting season and the summer sawmill work when the shanty boys collected their final wages and flooded into Bay City for Hell's Week. Hired helpers met them and handed out tokens for free food and drink to lure the men to the Catacombs. This four square block area downtown stretched along the river and was packed with saloons, gambling houses, brothels, liquor stores, and apothecary shops connected by underground passages. At the time, Bay City had 162 saloons where the stench of smoke lingered with the rancid clothes of the shanty boys, and money poured from their pockets faster than liquor into their glasses.

With the overwhelming rush of workers migrating to town for Hell's Week, a day didn't go by without scores of men getting drunk, robbed, beaten, propositioned, or murdered. The police force (if fourteen volunteers could rightfully be called a force) tried its best to maintain order by arresting a few souls here and there, but the officers usually looked the other way as saloon owners slipped bribes into their hungry pockets and drinks into their thirsty hands. The only constant work for the police that week was dragging "floaters" out of the river. These dead bodies usually bobbed in the water for days, so bloated and decomposed they were impossible to identify.

Tekla's older brother, Stash, had made his living then

as a shanty boy and was often at the head of the pack rushing to the Catacombs for the week of hedonism. He usually started perched at a poker table with piles of chips in front of him. His reputation as a master bluffer was so intimidating many opponents folded away winning hands, unable to decipher his stoic face, those impenetrable black eyes and that smirk—an impish swirl that taunted men with its unwavering certainty and complete disdain for incompetence.

When he wasn't at the card table, Stash was sure to be flirting with the "pretty waiter girls" who were quick to seduce the men upstairs or out to any of the multiple brothels a short walk away. Prostitution was legal in Michigan before World War I, and the wildest brothel could be found on the edge of the river at Water Street and Third. Known to be the best peanut house in town, this boarding house offered more than little salty snacks to its clientele. For the lofty price of five dollars, men ventured up to the third floor and watched women in scandalous outfits performing the raunchiest of acts.

It wasn't just the debauchery upstairs that drew men to this peanut house. Nightly bareknuckled bouts in the basement attracted standing room only crowds. Stash, with his towering frame and lumberjack build, was a favorite at the fights, and there wasn't a local pugilist who could knock him to the ground. Through the constant flow of migrating workers, Stash's reputation quickly spread by word of mouth. Challengers from all across the state flocked to the area during Hell's Week to take on this invincible fighter. Soon, the bouts became an unofficial contest where men vied for the reputed honor of tough man of Bay City. Stash took on all comers and defeated them decisively. After collecting the prize money, he was one of the few men to finish the seven days of pleasure with cash still in his pocket.

By Sunday night, the shanty boys were exhausted,

bruised, and hungover, but they had little time to recover from their pains. The next morning, sawmill supervisors opened the doors at five-thirty for the first shift of the season. If the lumberjacks wanted a guaranteed job for the summer, they showed up with their mouths shut, ready for the grueling work ahead of them. For the rest of the season, the men spent their lunch breaks bragging about their exploits from Hell's Week, topping each other's stories and fantasizing about what they'd do next year.

Stash often had some of the most memorable tales, but there was one story he never told anyone. Only his friends who were there with him knew. It was an evening like most during those reckless summers in the basement of the peanut house, where the cheers and curses mixed with the ripe stench of ale and sweat. On this particular night in 1888, five drunk bruisers from out of town swaggered into the brawling area, eager to take on the tough man of Bay City. The boldest of the group, a husky, scarred man who had spent most his life fighting, pulled a crumpled wad of bills from his pocket and accepted any bets that the Bay City fighter couldn't take on all five of them. The rowdy spectators urged Stash to accept the challenge.

He looked at the five opponents, and that smirk spread across his lips.

Roars and taunts filled the room as odds were yelled out. Seven to one! Ten to one! Twenty to one! Bets were made whether all five men would last, whether two, three, or four of them could take Stash down. Clyde Danka served as the timekeeper and explained that he'd signal another challenger in every thirty seconds. No weapons were allowed, but all other means of attack were permitted, and encouraged.

The boldest man stepped into the marked ring, cracked his neck to both sides, and motioned he was ready. Clyde rang the bell, and Stash charged the man, catching him by surprise. He headbutted him and landed four quick punches to his nose. The man fell to his knees, spit out two teeth, and collapsed to the ground. Two spectators dragged his body out of the ring.

All in less than ten seconds.

The packed audience erupted with deafening cheers as Clyde motioned the next man into the ring. The stout opponent gulped as the color faded from his face. The challenger advanced toward Stash and swung with all his might, but Stash sidestepped the punch and slapped the man in the back of the head. Insults and laughter bellowed from the audience, and Stash threw three, four, five jabs to the opponent's kidneys. He spun him around and delivered an uppercut to his stomach, knocking the wind out of him. The man dropped to the floor, and the third man, sinewy in stature but ravenous with attack, rushed in before Clyde signaled. He pounded Stash across the back of the neck. Stash swiveled around and caught the attacker by the throat and, in one swift motion, swept him from his feet and slammed him to the dirt floor. He drove his elbow into the man's chest repeatedly until he wailed for mercy.

Stash sprang to his feet, anticipating the fourth man to rush in early, but the girthy man waved off the challenge, not willing to endure Stash's attack.

Clyde lifted Stash's arms victoriously into the air and called the fight over. Lappie and Duyser patted Stash on the back and the gamblers collected money from the losers.

The fifth man, the drunkest runt of the group, stepped into the ring. "The fight's na ova," he slurred to the crowd. "I gotta chans. I gotta chans!"

Stash dismissed this challenge with a wave of his hand.

"I ga," the measly man pulled up his sleeve. "I ga a

silva watch, a solid silva watch, ta anyone who'll gimme, gimme forty-ta-one odds. Anyone? A solid silva watch."

A few muffled laughs sparked throughout the room, then Herbert Henderson stepped forward and accepted the bet. The audience erupted with yells and hoots, and the challenger struggled to pull his shirt over his head, revealing his flabby chest. He staggered around, punching the air, while Stash remained with his arms at his side, shaking his head. The man advanced toward him, fists drawn, swinging and dodging, his punches not even coming close. Stash stared the man down, leaving his body open. The scrawny fellow threw a fury of slaps to Stash's chest and midsection. Each blow landed with little force. Stash shoved the man back, and he crashed to the floor. The spectators taunted the little guy, urging him to slap harder, to pinch more. The drunk man cursed them and scrambled to his feet, yelling at Stash to fight like a man and throw a punch.

But Stash just stood there, shaking his head, as that disrespecting smirk crept across his face.

The challenger couldn't take it any longer. He rushed forward and jabbed his thumb into Stash's left eye. Stash doubled over and held his face, groaning in pain. The man spat on Stash's neck and rammed his elbow into the side of Stash's head. Stash reeled, disoriented, struggling to see with his good eye, but the challenger hovered in his blind spot and drove his boot into Stash's knee. His leg buckled, and he limped painfully, jerking around to see his assailant as yells and whistles echoed off the walls.

Then in one twirl, Stash spotted the man and roared his arm back. It connected with brutal force. The man's head snapped to the side, and his limp neck pulled his body to the floor.

Stash didn't notice the spectators empty out of the basement as he shuffled forward, rubbing the sting from his eye. He dropped to his knees in front of the man and shook him.

Not a twitch, not a jerk, not a breath.

Stash struck the body's chest, screaming to the man whose name he didn't know. He beat down over and over, trying to pound the life back into him. Four men pulled Stash back and urged him to grab the man's legs. They hoisted the flaccid body from the floor, and someone opened the basement door leading to the underground tunnels. A single torch led the men down the dank Catacomb passageway, and Stash followed behind them, unable to look away from the body, muttering that its eyes were moving in the flickering light. His fellow lumberjacks insisted that he continue on, and the passage soon opened near the river bank. The men dragged the body to its edge, but Stash stopped them, mumbling how the body deserved a proper burial, how they should take it to the police.

The other men said nothing.

Stash looked each of them in the eye and knew they were willing to help him, but that was asking too much. He nodded and understood what had to be done.

He squatted beside the body, and Lappie and Duyser stepped forward, but Stash stopped them with his hand. He lifted the dead weight himself, carried it to the river's edge, and heaved the body out. The corpse splashed into the placid surface, bobbing face-up in the wake. Stash waited for it to sink, but the body held its spot, floating on the moonlit reflection. He couldn't take his eyes off the dead man slinking across the rippling waves, drifting back to the shore, back to him. He stretched his leg out and pushed the body away. It surged from the bank, hovering a few yards offshore, but the corpse refused to sink, and slowly it crept back toward Stash.

He waded into the waist-high river and grabbed the body's bare shoulders and shoved the corpse under water. Bubbles rushed to the river's surface, and Stash held the body submerged for a full minute after the air stopped rising from its lungs. He released the corpse and let the undercurrents of the river carry the floater away.

Stash stepped toward the bank and grabbed the offered hand that helped him out of the water.

"Stash, it's not—"

"Don't." Stash pointed his finger at the man. "Don't."

His friends understood his unspoken order, and Stash waved them away. Each man lingered for a few moments, then headed off in a different direction away from the peanut house.

Stash walked the seven miles home, his soaked jeans hardening in the night air. There, he threw back shot after shot of vodka until the memory of the body bobbing in the river washed away from his mind.

6

Tavo Guerra knew what it was like to watch a man die. To see him struggling to pry clenched fingers from around his neck, straining to suck in a breath before his eyes finally rolled back into his head. It was something Tavo never did for pleasure, only for business. He had found no better way to ensure that the field hands paid for the booze, dice, and women he provided at his cantina just north of the Mexico border.

Half a mile from the fields, he had converted an old stable into a gambling hall, complete with rooms upstairs and a saloon packed with tequila and mezcal shipped in from Mexico. There, English mingled with Spanish, and little was understood between the *gringos* and the Mexican workers. Occasionally, miscommunications erupted into fistfights, but Tavo's bouncers were quick to regain control by breaking a nose or tearing off an ear. Tavo insisted they never touch a man's limbs. He respected an honest day's work and prided himself on injuries that ensured the worker would be back in the field the next day, no matter how deformed his face.

This intimidating, dark-skinned man patrolled his gambling hall with the watchful eye and precise gait of an iguana. No one knew exactly where this thirty-year-old, mustached Mexican was from, but nobody really cared as long as the cantina stayed open. Most of the field hands were on Tavo's good side, which meant they owed him money. And that guaranteed Tavo was watching their backs, whether they wanted him to or not.

Tavo collected the till from the bartender, finished his hourly patrol, and stepped out of the cantina. He rolled a cigarette under the silent Texas night and walked across the compound to the barracks where the workers rented bunks. His ears perked up as an excited voice rose from an open window. Tavo sat down on the bench beneath the screen, took a long drag off his cigarette, and listened to the conversation.

"You should see him at the plate. He bats like nobody else, spreading his hands far apart like this, and hits the ball wherever he wants. Highest average in the league for the second year in a row. And eleven seasons in a row before that. Mark my word, he will be the greatest player of all time."

A few disinterested listeners grunted in response.

"I remember stories about him," the voice continued. "The new kid from the South. The Georgia Peach was what they called him. He was no more than sixteen or seventeen when Detroit picked him up. I knew how good he was and told my friends at Pulaski's. They said I was crazy. But I told them I would name my first son after him to prove it. They laughed, but I was right. I was right."

"Cobb ain't that good," another voice contested.

"That is crazy talk."

"He's lost every World Series he's been in."

"The rest of his teammates, gypsies," the voice retorted. "Every one of them. He is still the greatest player in the league."

"Cobb's on a losing team," a third voice jabbed. "and that's all that's true."

"You do not know what you are saying."

Tavo inhaled the last of his cigarette and flicked the butt into the clearing as the futile argument volleyed back and forth. He stood up, walked to the back entrance, and let himself in.

Kowalczyk stopped mid-sentence.

Tavo glared at him. "People are sick of your *Tigres*, Janowicz."

Kowalczyk said nothing and rose to his feet as the other two men hustled out of the barracks.

Tavo motioned with his finger for Kowalczyk to sit back down. "Why are you not at the cantina tonight?" He walked toward Kowalczyk's bunk. "For a week you don't go."

"I do not feel good."

"*Mentiroso*. Don't lie to me. You look fine."

"I am saving money. To pay you back."

"Your credit is good. No need to worry."

"No. No more."

"What? My money is no good for you?"

"No, it is. I do not want more debt."

Tavo stepped beside Kowalczyk and towered over him. He reached behind his back. "Do you plan to run, Janowicz?"

"Why do you say that? I will pay you."

"*Bueno*. Then come and play."

"I can not lose more," Kowalczyk whined.

Tavo pulled a knife from his back pocket and extended the sharp blade. He ran his thumb thoughtfully over its edge. "I give you good deal, no?"

"Yes, you are very kind."

"I let you pay me once a week because you keep playing, *sí*?"

"Yes."

"That is our deal. You play, you pay me a little each week."

"I do not have the money yet."

Tavo snatched Kowalczyk's hand and slammed it against the wall, pressing a blade against his palm. "Play or pay, Janowicz, *entienda*?"

Kowalczyk clenched his teeth and nodded quickly as his eyes teared up.

"'*Stabien*. Later tonight, *sí*?"

"Yes. Yes, I will be there."

"When?"

"Later tonight."

Tavo tossed Kowalczyk's hand to the side. "Good. We understand. I won't speak of this again."

7

He dashed past his mother out of the house.

"Ty, your lunch."

"I'll have it later," he yelled back. His mother called out, but he didn't hear a word as he darted into the barn and closed the door behind him.

The sweet smell of varnish and sawdust mixed with the hazy shafts of light that hung from the cracks in the roof. The electric table saw kept him from his meals. The sandpaper and stain deprived him of sleep. The tool-covered workbenches lured him back repeatedly. This was Ty's place, his home where he crafted shapeless pieces of wood into furniture. To take something without purpose and create it into something that did, that was the power of a god. His mother always scolded him for his excessive pride, but, in Ty's mind, that wasn't a bad thing. It was empowering, freeing. But, as of late, Ty was spending less and less time filling those five orders Uncle Stash was waiting for. Something else occupied his mind.

Ty moved to the back corner of the barn where a black cloth tarp was arranged so inconspicuously that no visitor would notice the pile beneath it. He fished out two pieces of wood: one expertly carved with flutes and curves; the other only vaguely resembling the same shape, two of its sides still flat. Its completion was still days away.

Ty inspected the finished piece, feeling every contour with his black eyes. He picked up the crude block

and whittled stroke after stroke, carving the unnecessary wood away, releasing the beautiful leg that the lumber contained.

The front door of the barn squeaked open, and Ty
stuffed the pieces back under the tarp. He scrambled
away from the corner.

Uncle Franek emerged from the shadows.

"Oh. It's you," Ty said.

"Don't let me interrupt you."

Ty grabbed an unsanded panel from the table and
sat on the bench against the wall.

His uncle walked to the middle of the barn and inspected a finished table next to the saw. "Your father'll
be proud of everyone talking about your work. You've
made quite a name for him."

Ty didn't look up.

"You look tired," his uncle commented.

"I'm fine."

"Health is important during the busy season."

"I said I'm fine."

"Good." His uncle stepped over to the carving table
and picked up an etched board. "People have stopped
by my store and asked about your tables."

"Send them here. Me and Uncle Stash will take their
orders."

Anger simmered in Uncle Franek's eyes.

"We won't sell to you again," Ty stated.

His uncle forced a smile. "I'm not asking you to."

"Just say it. You're not happy we're doing good on
our own."

"I am happy for you, Ty. Your father and I trust whatever you do. But he asked me to keep an eye on his
business, and I want to make sure you understand the
risk you're taking."

"Risk? What are you talking about?"

Uncle Franek sat down across from Ty.

"I see the sparkle in your eye when you talk about selling your pieces. Making more money than you can believe, yes?"

Ty nodded.

"But what will happen when this selling spree ends? How will you make money then?"

"You're trying to scare me."

"Believe what you want, but you're family, and I'm trying to help. For years I've run my store and had plenty of good streaks. But I've had bad ones too. Very bad. Have you considered that?"

Ty shrugged.

His uncle leaned forward. "See, you've only experienced the good side of business. You can't have one without the other. Your father knows that. Years ago, when you were small, he almost lost everything."

"No, he didn't."

"He did. You probably never heard because he didn't want to worry you or your mother. But you should know since you're becoming a man with a say in your father's business."

"You only care about your store and taking the money from father that he rightfully earned."

"Why do you say that?"

"I know."

"Your Uncle Stash tells you this? Or your mother?"

Ty looked away.

"They don't know the whole story," he stressed. "Before the timber industry crashed and everyone lost their jobs, your father spent many nights at Pulaski's gambling. But he rarely won. Then the lumber disappeared, and everyone was hit hard. The South End. The West Side. Banks. Essexville. Even along Center, people struggled. Nobody had money for new furniture, so your father came to me and asked for help. He was family, so I helped. We made an agreement that during good times

31

and bad, I would buy tables from him."

"You stole from him."

"No, I guaranteed your father a paycheck. I kept food on your table and a roof over your head. Yes, at times I gave him less, but your father always had money."

"I don't believe you."

"Why would I lie? He wanted the arrangement. If he was here, he'd tell you. But he isn't. So it's up to you to decide."

"I've made my decisi—"

"Let me finish." His uncle sat up. "I understand you don't want to sell your tables to me. I don't agree with that, but I'll respect your decision. But you're breaking an agreement your father and I have had for over fifteen years. You want more profits, that's fine. But I'm not going to wait for you to change your mind and sell to me again. I've gone two months now without pieces, and I have to find someone to fill my orders. Don't be fooled. This will be easy for me, four carpenters have already knocked on my door. But I can only pay one builder, and I won't buy tables from you or your father again."

"We don't need your money."

"Ideally, no. But what happens when those bad times return? Because they always do. When families can't afford fancy, hand-carved tables, who will buy your pieces then? Who will save your father's business next time? A business he's labored on for years. Will you take that risk?"

Ty glared at his uncle.

"I'll give you another three days to think about it."

"I know now."

"I will not be the one to break this news to your father when he returns." Uncle Franek rose from the bench. "I'll check with you on Thursday." He let himself out of the barn.

"I won't sell to you," Ty yelled after him. "I won't!"

Ty tore into the wooden piece in his hand, sanding it down until his anger faded and the abrasive paper slowed to a stop. Ty glanced around at the work areas, at the saw and the lumber, at the planes and the drills, at the cans of stain and the brushes, and took a deep, pensive breath.

8

They had done just as their son had instructed. They packed father's long coat and mother's full-brimmed hat into a handbag. They borrowed the automobile from their neighbor Mr. Rozanski. They arrived at Pere Marquette Railroad Depot at half past eleven Saturday night. Then they waited.

Ana Sinicki clutched her husband's hand and held sobs deep in her throat. Henrik squeezed back and fought off his own tears. He patted her hand, grabbed the handbag, and walked to the train station doors.

The lobby was empty, silent in the darkness of night. Only the flickering of a few electric lights hummed overhead. Portraits hung from the wall like epitaphs. Leon Trobley. Albert Miller. James Fraser. The original settlers of Bay City. Each painting of a time long ago, before the war had made things so complex. Henrik's stomach tightened as he heard a train approaching. He swallowed hard and slid the handbag beneath the corner bench against the far wall. Then Henrik fled back to his wife.

Ten minutes passed. A figure cloaked in the overcoat and hat emerged from the depot doors. An army duffle bag hung from its shoulder. Henrik eased out of the car and waved to his son, who nodded and headed toward him. Ignasiu handed his bag to his father and helped himself into the back seat without a word. Full sobs broke from Ana, and she turned around and clasped her hands around her son's neck. She tried to pull him near, but

Ignasiu jerked back. He adjusted the large hat over his face with his right hand.

Henrik got into the car, grabbed his wife's hand, and started the vehicle for home.

9

When the U.S. entered the Great War, the government offered lucrative contracts to businesses to manufacture military supplies. Shell casings. Stretchers. Leather boots. Blankets. Helmets. Gas lanterns. Tin dishes. Buckles. Knife blades. Canvas tents. Everything the American troops needed. Wilson's Body Shop originally molded steel into automobile bumpers, but the company received a contract to convert its metal warehouse into a sewing factory. Notices had been sent to the South End for any women interested in positions. Hundreds showed up the next morning. Tekla Kowalczyk was sixteenth in line, and her knowledge of sewing and carpentry qualified her for a position. Fifty hours a week, stitching fabric together and stretching it over the wooden wing frames of DH-4s.

Playing a direct role in the lives of the U.S. pilots and soldiers, the women dove into the initial months of work with a mixture of apprehension and pride. But as more and more employees found their own husbands, sons, and brothers shipped off to war, the mood rose and fell with the developments at the front. As new orders surged into the plant, the women feared many American pilots were being shot down. When new orders lagged, they rejoiced, hoping the war was nearing its end. But they secretly worried that their jobs would be given away to the returning soldiers.

A day didn't go by at the shop without someone asking Tekla if she'd heard new information from

Andrzej. She could only shake her head and offer a wrinkle of a smile. People didn't believe her silence and pried to know what she was hiding. They became more persistent, backing her into corners, questioning her about her husband, as if their lives depended upon the details.

But why Andrzej Kowalczyk?, Tekla wondered.

With all of the other Polish men serving in Europe, why did people revere her husband? He wasn't the most competent person nor the most handsome, and he was years beyond his prime. Yet he was a hero to many in the South End. Perhaps it *was* because Andrzej was so unheroic that he was the obvious choice. No matter how dire their own situations, if someone like Andrzej Kowalczyk could rise to great heights, so could they. Tekla never believed any of the rumors circulating about her husband's secret mission in Europe. She felt the stories were being created by the very people who wanted to hear them. How pitiful to believe so passionately in her husband's exploits. But who was she to take away that hope from the people of the South End?

This pity she felt for others, though, didn't compare to the dread those same people felt for her. Often when friends and co-workers thought she was out of earshot, Tekla overheard them debating whether she could handle the time without her husband. It would be too much for her, they worried. Actually, Tekla was ecstatic to gain the freedoms and opportunities from the war and Andrzej's departure. Now she had a job and was able to run the woodworking business as she saw fit.

But these freedoms hadn't been available with Andrzej around. Tekla was only fourteen when she was married off to a man ten years her elder. At that age, she silenced her questions about her husband's decisions and didn't wonder if he was wrong. Her own father's carpentry business was managed masterfully. With Stash working in the forest and her mother deceased, Tekla played an essential role in her father's success. She was responsible for cooking, cleaning, carving, sanding, sewing, mending, building, sawing, gardening, washing, delivering. There wasn't a job around the house or barn that Tekla couldn't do. Her father told her what he needed help with, and she did it. And his business was prosperous.

So when Andrzej forbade Tekla from working in the barn that first year of their marriage, she couldn't understand his reasoning. He must have his own effective method of running his business, she thought, and I'll be worked into his system over time. That never happened. Over the years, Tekla grew less and less confident with Andrzej's decisions and skills. The way he kowtowed to Franek and followed his every demand made no sense to her. When her husband pulled Ty out of school, she wanted to protest but saw how necessary it was. Andrzej had fallen so far behind with orders, even if she had forced him to allow her to work in the barn, the two of them wouldn't have been enough. They needed Ty out there all day, seven days a week. For two months, Ty labored sixteen hours a day, helping Andrzej make tables. Franek bought none. Tekla remembered Ty begging his father to let him carve intricate designs into the pieces, but Andrzej refused. A table is made simply, he barked, and that is the only way. That was the last time her husband allowed the topic to be mentioned. Three weeks later, frustrated with his own incompetence, Andrzej accused the family of not working hard enough and yanked a sobbing Stanley from school.

That was unacceptable.

Tekla should have stopped him. She could sand and stain and carve just as easily. She should have insisted Stanley stay in school, but she didn't offer a single word of protest.

For weeks Tekla cursed herself for her lack of assertion, but once Andrzej left for training in Texas, she met with Miss Noonan and got Stanley back in the classroom. Now Ty built tables the way he wanted to. Stash delivered orders. Stanley sanded and stained every afternoon. And after her shifts at Wilson's, Tekla picked up the slack wherever help was needed. Her system was flawless.

She just hoped Andrzej would continue to let things run as smoothly if he ever returned.

10

He sat at his desk Thursday afternoon, pencil in hand, drawing circles, aimless circles in the margins of his ledger. He had grown sick of calculating the columns, always finding the debits exceeding the credits. Extra merchandise crowded his packed floor. Rash purchases had been returned. Orders were shipped out that had never been paid for. Pieces lingered that nobody would ever buy, no matter how much the prices were cut. That was what Franek's store had become.

Many local families owed him loan payments but couldn't scrape together enough for the monthly bill. These families, however, weren't really the problem; they had solid roots in the South End and weren't going to move away. The transient shipyard workers with their desperate stories and sincere promises were a different situation. Franek had grown greedy at the end of the summer and made a handful of loans at high interest rates to workers. The payments were supposed to start coming in with their weekly checks, but four of the five men fled Bay City without paying back a cent. Their allegedly sentimental collateral barely covered a fraction of the advance.

Franek rose from his chair and roamed the aisles of beds and chairs and pots and pans and bureaus and chests and kitchenware. Everything a family needed, all in one store. That had been the key to Franek's success. Now these items could be found anywhere. Traveling by trolley car to any of the other neighborhoods in

Bay City cost only a few cents. Even the new stretch of shops opening along Tittabawassee Road in Saginaw was a quick, cheap trip. And the few buyers who still trickled into Franek's shop seemed to only want to see Ty's tables. Those moments took every ounce of will for Franek to restrain his brewing anger.

Franek ran his hand through his thinning, silver hair and checked his watch. It was almost time to meet his nephew. Franek had little hope that Ty had changed his mind, so he grabbed his hat and headed to Pulaski's for a drink first.

Franek stepped inside the Hall and felt the hot air push laughter and conversation against his face. He hung his hat on the wooden peg by the door and greeted a few men with a nod. Franek navigated through the crowds toward the bar and ordered a beer.

A drunken Jan Zubek turned to Franek and snarled. "What makes your brother so God damn special? My son's in Europe, and nobody talks about him."

Franek didn't have the energy to reply. He grabbed his mug and stepped away.

"He's a hero too," Zubek shouted after him.

Franek moved to a table and heard his name called from the side. Isaak Sawicki, the cobbler from 35th Street, chuckled, pointing his way. The other men at the table turned in Franek's direction and suppressed their laughter.

Franek walked over to them. "Good evening, Sawicki. What's so funny?"

"Nothing, Franek."

"It is nothing," Matuszewski said, dismissing the question with a wave of his hand.

"Your business is good, yes?" Owsiak asked.

The table exploded with laughter as the men exchanged knowing glances.

Franek tried to read their faces. "Why do you ask?"

"We hear of competition for you."

"Yes, tough competition from up the road."

"I don't know what you mean," Franek said.

"This afternoon. Ty came in for a drink."

"He's a good boy. He bought everyone a glass."

"Vodka for everyone."

"That is good," Franek said. "The boy is finally old enough to—"

"Then he stood up," Matuszewski blurted out, "and called our attention. Brozewski stopped his accordion, and everyone listened. He climbed on a chair and said, 'I make the best tables in the South End. In the entire town. Now I am in business for myself. A toast to me and my father. My uncle will no longer carry my tables. If you want the best, come to me. As a bonus, orders made before mass on Sunday will be delivered by Thanksgiving. That is my promise to you. From the best woodsmith in the South End.' And we drank to the newest Polish businessman."

"That boy is a gypsy, I tell you," Sawicki claimed, "but he makes the best damn tables I ever saw."

"What will you sell now, Franek?"

"That boy has no need for an aging uncle."

Snickers flared among the men.

Franek smiled as sincerely as he could. "Ty and I spoke of this before. We decided it was the best for both of us."

Three of the men restrained their laughter.

"Sure you did Franek."

Franek nodded and ordered a round of drinks for the table to celebrate the arrangement. He sat down and tried to mask his emotions with smiles and toasts. Around eleven Franek excused himself and wished the men good night. An ovation of mocking cheers and applause sent him off. Franek snatched his hat from the peg, knowing his show of indifference had convinced no one. He would never forgive this disgrace to his reputation.

11

Sweat dripped from Andrzej Kowalczyk's body as he dropped his final sack of onions off at the barn. For six nights now, since Tavo's visit, Kowalczyk had been at the card table in the saloon, trying to whittle down his debt. Each night he added to his amount, pushing it to insurmountable figures.

He wiped his face with his shirt and trudged to the foreman's shack behind the storage building and knocked on the door. He pulled it open and stepped inside.

"I didn't say come in," his boss lashed from the small desk in the back. He snatched the stacks of money before him, stuffed them into a cigar box, and stuck it into the top desk drawer.

Kowalczyk stood in silence.

"What do you want, Janowicz?"

"I will give you half my pay for a daily advance."

The foreman stared at Kowalczyk. "Fine. Pick it up tomorrow after your shift."

"I would prefer to start today."

"I don't have the money now."

Kowalczyk motioned with his head toward the desk drawer. "You just put it away, sir."

The foreman paused. "If you tell anyone I'm doing this for you, your job's done. Understand?"

"Yes, sir. No one will know."

The foreman pulled the cigar box from the drawer and counted out half a day's wage and tossed it onto the desk. "Now, get outta here."

12

To the untrained customer, there is little difference between the kinds of wood used to build a house, a carriage wheel, or a kitchen chair. Usually whatever is cheapest and available is sufficient. But anyone who makes woodworking a part of his life knows that this is far from the truth. The type of timber you pick depends upon the project at hand.

Michigan's most famous tree, the pine, is a superb outdoor lumber; it's quick to dry and effective for building any house or barn. Black locust has strength and resilience and makes excellent fence posts and railroad tracks. To build a durable wagon wheel, combine the strong flexibility of ash for the outer rim and the shock resistance of hickory for its spokes and axle. Elm decays quickly if allowed to dry, but if kept constantly damp, it will last forever, which is why it's the choicest timber for water pipes. Bendable osage orange is best for hunting bows, sculptable basswood for any cigar store Indian or seaward figurehead, rot-free willow for artificial limbs, and maple for butcher blocks. Apple is effective for wooden screws or nuts, birch for kitchen plates, bowls, and spoons, sassafras for ox yokes, and red cedar is claimed to ward off moths.

Now these types of lumber are important for any woodsmith to know, but Ty built most of his pieces from the finer furniture woods. Black cherry with its beautiful reddish-brown finish. Imported mahogany burns a rich brownish-red. And walnut offers a brownish-gray with streaks of purple. But these weren't hidden beneath the tarp in the back corner. There, Ty had the king of all woods, wood that even the most ignorant of customers would know: oak.

Oak has the strength like no other wood and can be used in nearly every building situation. Most seafaring men toast white oak as the best around. It's impervious to water and can endure all weather conditions, which makes it the reigning king of whiskey barrels and ship hulls. Furniture makers prefer red oak. This lumber is vulnerable to water and decay, but if it's used for indoor furniture, there's nothing better. It's a challenge to carve, but the finished work makes the effort worthwhile.

Ty's ears perked up as he heard Uncle Stash's voice calling his name from the clearing. Dammit, Ty thought, those five orders. He shoved the oak pieces back under the tarp and cluttered some tools and scraps around the area. Ty hustled to the carving table on the other side of the barn and picked up a hunk of lumber to busy himself.

The front barn door flew open, and Uncle Stash raced in, waving slips of paper in his hand.

"Ty, Ty! What have you done? So many orders."

"How many, Uncle? How many?"

"Dozens."

Ty took the slips and began counting.

"People knocked on my door last night. They met me outside the shipyards this morning. My supervisor called me into his office during break."

"Sixteen orders, Uncle."

"Sixteen orders," Stash gasped in disbelief.

"Yes, and two more days to go."

"That's more than we can handle."

"It'll be easy."

"Before Thanksgiving? Ty, that's impossible. I can't help any more than I do now."

"I don't expect you to. I'll complete the orders."

"You have the pride of a gypsy. You make beautiful

tables that people want, that they'd be willing to wait for. Why do you make this extra pressure?"

"It's no problem. I've thought this through many times. You cut the pieces. I carve the designs. Stanley sands and varnishes. And mother puts them together."

"But carving takes the longest. You're the only one with enough time to do it."

Ty dismissed the comment with a wave. "It won't take long. Tell those sixteen orders they'll be finished by Thanksgiving."

———————

Word spread throughout the Polish community about the boy who promised the tables. At church. At the general store. In the shipyards. The Wisinskis and Hryniewiczs from 32nd Street jumped at the opportunity. As did the Czarneckis on 16th Street and the Wituckis on Cass Avenue.

Most others didn't believe the claim. It is just a trick, they thought, to bring more customers to their business. A table of that quality, of that design, couldn't be sold for that low. It is barely possible to buy a regular table at that price. But that was the guarantee made by the Kowalczyk boy. Have you heard about his skills? His tables are already in a few estates on Center Avenue. On Center Avenue? Yes, Jarik Wolczyk swears by it. Are you sure? Yes. Our family is as good as any on Center. There is no reason we shouldn't own one. And the Janczyks placed their order.

They're promised by Thanksgiving, or else they're free. Free? That's his promise, all before Thanksgiving. And only a small deposit is needed to secure your purchase. The rest is due on delivery. It's too good to be believed. A table from the Kowalczyk boy. And the Kuczynskis told Stash what they wanted.

We'd be foolish not to take advantage of that deal. Even with the restrictions on Meatless Mondays and Wheatless Wednesdays, things are better for us. Mother and little Rebeka have good jobs. And with the Americans pushing the German forces back, the war will be over in no time. The soldiers will return home and take back the jobs. An opportunity to buy such a fine table at a low price may never come again. And the Janiszewskis paid their deposit.

The Izydoreks and Niedzwickis each debated about getting a coffee table. The Furtows needed to replace the two end tables in their living room. The Czaplas discussed buying a dining room table for their daughter Basha who would be married in the spring. The Zielinskis wondered if the Kowalczyk boy would be willing to build them a desk. And the Pawickis hoped to get a dresser.

By Sunday morning, twenty-six more orders were placed. During the pastor's sermon about the carpenter's son, Ty grinned and stared out the window, thinking about how his father's business was on the verge of becoming one of the most profitable in the entire city.

13

Andrzej Kowalczyk swung his legs over the edge of his bunk and glanced around the room, making sure no one was around. He slid over and unlocked the footchest where he kept his belongings. There wasn't much inside. Some shirts, a few folded socks, underclothing. Kowalczyk searched through the garments and fished out a pair of balled socks. Inside was a crumpled envelope. He stuffed that into his pocket, relocked the chest, and stole away into the night.

The clearing on the other side of the barracks was a common meeting place for the workers who needed a break from Tavo's. Rusted-out barrels fencepoled the area and brewed with flames that illuminated the gathered men. Kowalczyk stood on the periphery, not wanting to break their camaraderie of complaints and frustrations.

It wasn't that Kowalczyk saw himself above these disappointed men. On the contrary, his own misdirected dreams and aimless hopes made him realize that their lives were no different than his. Marty Rosewell longed to own his own business in Austin, but resigned himself to picking crops for the last six years. Leo Milton spoke of courting the woman he loved in New Orleans, but did little to convince her by spending a fourth year in Texas. Andrzej wanted to be a war hero but was on the verge of letting months of field work become the rest of his life. He had to break free.

A group of harvesters drifted away from a barrel.

Kowalczyk moved beside the bonfire and pulled the crumpled envelope from his pocket. He had read the words from the letter inside only once, months ago, but the message wouldn't leave him. Kowalczyk had tried exhaustively to forget what it said, but the more he struggled to erase the exact words, the more the message etched into his consciousness.

> *physical aptitude prevents . . . reassigned . . .*
> *homefront duty . . . two weeks to report to*
> *South Carolina . . .*

How could he impress Franek with such a disgrace?

So Andrzej Kowalczyk ran away from training camp and traveled as far south as his money would take him. McAllen, Texas. There, he asked around for work, and a withered man pointed to a road that led to fields where they always needed extra hands. Kowalczyk thanked him and hiked the three miles east. That would be the perfect job, he thought, one he could hold for a day or two, a week at the most, before heading to Carolina.

When the foreman asked him his name, Andrzej Kowalczyk—as if he already knew he wasn't going to head to the east coast—gave a fake name. Not really a fake name, but the first one that popped into his head. Janowicz. Stanislaw Janowicz. Stash for short, his brother-in-law's name.

Kowalczyk dangled the crumpled envelope over the flames until a spark ignited the lower corner. The sizzling glow ate its way along the edge of the paper, and Andrzej dropped the envelope into the fire and watched the flames incinerate the dishonor. But the image of that fiery letter and its content were burned into his mind forever.

14

Ty jolted awake and dropped the carving knife to the ground. His mouth clamped over the pain on the back of his hand, and he sucked blood from the deep gash below his wrist. He grabbed the cleanest rag he could find and pressed it against his hand, cursing his clumsiness and exhaustion.

It was only recently that Ty had noticed his reflection in the mirror and how the lack of sleep and nourishment affected him. But his reflection didn't concern him the way it bothered his mother. That was only physical fatigue. As long as his mind was sharp, his exhausted body was inconsequential.

Insomnia was nothing new to Ty. He had experienced it for most of his life. On most nights, he'd drag his body to bed and collapse on top of the covers, letting his head sink into the pillow. But the moment his eyelids closed, his body had lost. His mind would envision a particular block of wood and strips of unnecessary lumber would peel away until it freed an exquisite shape. Then another carved piece would appear and connect perfectly with the first. Then another connected to the first two, and so on, until a completed desk or armoire or dresser materialized in his mind. At that point, Ty knew he was beyond sleep. So he'd roll over and stare at the ceiling or gaze out the window as hours crawled by.

Over the last couple months, Ty had decided to make use of his sleepless nights. Instead of lying awake in bed, Ty would get out from under the covers, move to the kitchen, and stoke the glowing embers of the stove. Then he'd grab a piece of scrap wood and whittle. Often only for twenty minutes, other times he'd last for hours, and sometimes until dawn. Regardless of how much time he spent, Ty felt relieved to be productive.

Ty glanced under the rag and saw the cut was still bleeding. He tied the cloth around his hand as Uncle Stash appeared from the threshold.

"Let's load those tables."

"They're not done."

"What?"

"The tables aren't done."

"You said they'd be finished today."

"I thought they would. A few more finishing touches. That's all."

"Klyachko and Laskowski are expecting deliveries today."

"I know," Ty stated. "I've just got to hammer one together and finish staining the other."

"Staining? That'll take all night to dry. These people have already paid us. They're expecting their furniture."

"They'll be done tomorrow."

"Klyachko's already given us three extra days. I can't ask him for more. What have you been doing?"

Ty shrugged. "Different projects."

"You don't have time for different projects. You knew these were due today."

"I know."

"How are we going to finish forty-two, if we can't complete the five orders we had before."

"I'll get them done." Ty escaped toward the varnish area. He grabbed a can of stain and jammed a screwdriver under the lid to pry it off. The can slipped from his wrapped hand, and the screwdriver head drove into the rag. Ty bit his lip, angry at himself.

Uncle Stash stepped over and picked up the can.

"You're right," Ty blurted. "I need to focus on those orders."

Stash looked at his bandaged hand. "You shouldn't let these tools treat you like that," he said with a grin.

Ty chuckled.

"What do you need me to do?"

Ty pointed with his head. "The last two legs are over there. You can attach them while I stain."

Uncle Stash popped the lid open and handed the can back to Ty.

15

Mrs. Sinicki carried the tray of kielbasa, czarnina, and rye rolls to the closed bedroom door. She didn't speak English and called out to her son in her native tongue, announcing his meal.

He didn't respond.

"Come to the door, Ignasiu," she pleaded, "and take your meal."

"Leave it on the floor," he answered in Polish.

Mrs. Sinicki stood there. "Come out of the room. For days you lock yourself in."

"Leave the food, mamusiu," he begged her. "You don't want to see me."

"Just once. To see your face."

"You don't, mamusiu. You don't."

Tears welled up in her eyes. She set the tray on the floor, pressed her hand against the door, and left her son alone.

16

Sandpaper scraped his knuckles. Sawdust irritated his eyes. Slivers pierced his palms. Errant hammers pounded his hand. Dropped boards smashed his toes. Copper wire, drill bits, spinning lathes, and chisels, all found their way into his flesh. For Ty, these occasional injuries were scarring his skin more and more frequently with the sheer exhaustion of his body.

But this pain didn't compare to what his father had endured, Ty thought. His father rarely spoke of it, but Ty knew from the stories his mother had told while he was growing up. Father's education had been given by Grandfather Vladimir in the family barn where they worked long days because God created bodies that could. Year after year, he strained every muscle and joint in his thin frame and worked as he was ordered. For nearly four decades, Ty's father had built coffee tables, dinner tables, end tables, bedside tables, and workbenches of all shapes, sizes, and designs, shipping them away to other people's houses. Building wasn't his father's passion, it was just a way to support his family. He never once made a table for himself.

After Grandfather Vladimir passed away, Uncle Franek started buying father's work but insisted on taking just his tables. And paid him only pittance for the pieces. Ty had seen it happen countless times and could hardly contain his rage. But often, his flares of anger weren't directed at his uncle, but at his own father. Ty despised how desperately he accepted this treatment without complaint. Father didn't need approval from his brother, but Ty sensed his father couldn't free himself from it. He wondered if this was the reason his father insisted on going off to war, years beyond when he should have enlisted. There were plenty of things people father's age could have done in Bay City to support the war campaign. He could have found something else to do other than build tables—

Thoughts like these made Ty grow hot with guilt, doubting his father's abilities. His ability to serve in the war, to make a quality table. Ty pushed those ideas far from his mind and found himself retreating to the hidden oak pieces. He had already measured out the space in the living room in front of the sofa where the table would stand. He imagined his father inviting guests to the house. They would gather around the cocktail table with their drinks and admire his father who would talk of his heroics in Europe. And after the parties were over, Ty and his father would work together again side by side, building and selling tables in direct defiance of Uncle Franek.

17

At eight forty-five every night, Ty would bring two stools next to the wood burning stove in the kitchen. There, he and his mother would sit, one on each side of the carving tools she had bought him years ago, and together they would practice sculpting basswood. Sometimes vehicles or humans or animals, other times fantastical creatures and objects never before seen. All the while, Stanley's typewriter pecked away in the background. They started this after father left for war, and it was the first time Ty noticed how talented his mother was as a woodworker. Over the months, he was amazed by her skills and aspired to match them. He couldn't understand why she hadn't been working in the barn while he was growing up.

Their latest game involved switching pieces midway through the process, when only a vague semblance of a figure existed, bodies and faces just beginning to take shape. With the exchanged piece in hand, Ty and his mother would either continue what the other person had started or take the piece in a completely different direction, adding new features or hacking off existing ones, until a new hybrid evolved. When Ty got back his original piece, his view of creative possibilities widened.

One night just after they had exchanged pieces, Ty stood up from his stool. He stared off and set his knife and basswood down, unaware his mother was waiting for an answer to her question.

"Ty," she called, "where are you going?"

"To the barn."

"You've worked all day. You need a break."

"I'll rest later." He stepped out of the house, walked across the yard, and pulled the barn door shut behind him, securing the latch.

He rested his palms and forehead against the door and closed his eyes. His lungs expanded deeply in his chest, and Ty held the breath as long as he could, hoping to calm the nerves in his stomach. Earlier Uncle Stash told him that Mr. Klyachko had cancelled his order and found a table elsewhere. How simple of an order to have let slip away. What was to follow?

Ty turned away from the door and ran his hands through his black hair, looking at the growing piles of cut legs and panels and sides and moldings and shelves. Pieces for the forty-two orders that couldn't be worked on by anybody but himself. They had to be carved before Stanley could sand or stain, before Uncle Stash could nail them together. He could ask his mother to help, but Ty didn't want her to know how much trouble he was in.

How many days had Ty just sat in the barn unable to work on anything? He knew what needed to be done. The piles glared at him daily and taunted his inactivity as they continued to grow. Still he could not will himself to work. The oak pieces and the guilty thoughts about his father distracted him. But that constant tingling in his stomach wouldn't let him forget that he had, perhaps, committed himself to more than he was capable. Making himself into a liar, a fraud. Forsaking his blossoming reputation because he flaunted more than he should.

Ty had sensed that even on the day he stood up in Pulaski Hall and promised tables to everyone. He was so eager to defy his uncle that he hadn't considered the previous orders nor the extra time he wanted to dedicate to his father's gift. Added to that, Ty anticipated getting many orders, but never in his wildest imagination had he thought so many would come from his announcement. It was amazing. It was exciting. It was impossible.

Now, he needed to focus all of his talent and energy, but he found little inspiration to fill those new orders. His bold promise had created an unnecessary trap, and Ty had placed his own neck into its jaws. His customers in the South End pressured him without even realizing it. The Wisinskis, Strukowskis, and Volczyks approached Ty in the streets. The Cianeks and Brokowskis spoke to him in the aisles before and after Mass on Sunday. And Pulaski Hall was the worst. Yesterday alone, Toporski, Hryniewicz, Sawicki, Sczesniak, Brozewski, and Matuszewski called Ty over to ask about their orders and designs. He answered their inquiries with vagaries, snuck out of the Hall, and retreated to the barn.

The looming deadline and multiplying piles continued to work against him. Ty spent hours staring at the untouched pieces until the unease in his stomach and the throbbing in his head became too much. Just the other day, Ty noticed the coughs sputtering from deep inside his lungs. Then, as he did now, he returned to the oak pieces and waited for the creative fury to seize his body and mind and propel him back to the growing piles.

18

Sometime after three in the morning, Andrzej Kowalczyk, panting rapidly, sweat streaming down his face, pounded on the front door of a house.

The door squeaked open. A young Mexican girl, no more than seventeen, stood, holding a lantern, trying to cover her naked body with a towel.

"Where is Tavo?"

She looked back incomprehensibly. "*Qué?*"

"Tavo. Is he here? Tavo."

"*Octavio? Sí.*"

She stepped aside and pointed down the hallway. Kowalczyk dashed past her into the darkness, and hands grabbed him by the chest and threw him face-first against the wall. The barrel of a pistol jammed into the back of his neck, cocked, ready to fire.

"Tavo?" he cried. "Tavo, it is me. Kowal—Janowicz."

The young girl floated into the hallway with the light, and Kowalczyk was flung around. A hand clutched his throat, the gun shoved into his cheek.

"What do you want?" Tavo stood bare-chested, unbuckled trousers around his waist.

"Your money. I have it."

Tavo barked to the girl in Spanish. She set the lantern on the floor and patted Kowalczyk's waist and pantlegs. Tavo ordered her again, and she dug into Kowalczyk's pocket and pulled out a wad of bills.

"That is all I owe," Kowalczyk stammered.

The girl offered the stack to Tavo, who checked it with his eyes. He jammed the pistol deeper into Andrzej's cheek.

"*Por qué?*"

"I have saved to pay you back."

"Pay me tomorrow. Just what you owe this week."

"I want to pay it all back."

A smile crept across Tavo's face. "You're going to run, Janowicz, aren't you?"

Kowalczyk feebly shook his head.

Tavo spoke to the girl, and she stuffed the bills into Kowalczyk's hand.

"Count it," Tavo ordered. "Let me see."

Kowalczyk showed each bill with his shaking hand. Six-hundred twenty-one dollars exactly. Tavo snatched the money and crammed it into his pocket. He slammed Kowalczyk's head against the wall and shoved the pistol into his temple. "I don't know where you got this money, Janowicz, but that is your problem. Not mine. *Entienda?*"

"It is my mon—"

"*Entienda?*" Kowalczyk's head bounced off the wall again.

"Yes. Yes. I understand."

"Get out of my house." Tavo threw him to the floor.

Kowalczyk scrambled to his feet and sprinted out into the night.

He ran as fast as his worn body could go, past the barracks and the chained, barking dogs, past the foreman's cabin and the fields, west down the three mile road until he arrived at the truck depot. Dozens of drivers were checking their trailers before they headed out for their daily hauls. He found a trucker going to Dallas who was happy to give him a ride. Andrzej Kowalczyk thanked him and leapt into his cab, hoping to get far away before the workers arrived for the morning shift.

Part Two

1

Years after the East Side had pocketed a windfall from the logging boom, the West Side of Bay City developed as an extension from the Henry Sage sawmill. Sage was a lumber baron to some, but to most of the shanty boys and their families, this absentee owner was a bandit. He funneled the vast profits from his lumberyard back to New York and did little to improve the workers' standard of living. The roads on the West Side were nothing more than mud slicks scarred with carriage ruts. Wooden sidewalks rotted away under the snow, rain, and humidity. And the shanty boys' makeshift shacks were a disgrace. When the timber finally ran out in 1888, so did the managers of the Sage mill, abandoning their affluent houses and the workers.

Over the next three decades, one area of the West Side grew into a vacation spot that lured families in from all across the state, and that was where the Kowalczyk boys were headed on Saturday morning. Stanley had been awake since five, anxiously waiting by the front door with a paper sack of rolls and hard-boiled eggs. He had been anticipating this day since Miss Noonan first pulled him aside three weeks ago and told him of the event. He skipped his paper route that day and rushed home to tell his brother the news. Ty promised to take him.

Unfortunately, this was well before the orders started flooding in, and Stanley didn't know that as his brother pulled himself out of bed that morning, Ty would have given anything to have this day to attack the ever-growing piles. But it wasn't Stanley's fault, Ty thought. He'd gotten himself into this situation and he wasn't going to break his promise to his younger brother. So without complaint or resentment, Ty set out from the house with Stanley to catch the seven-thirty bus at 32nd Street.

The bus motored along Water Street into the heart of the city where the trains and trolleys came together at Pere Marquette Station. From there it was a short walk down to the riverside where the steel skeleton of the Third Street Bridge slowly took shape and small ferries waited for cross-city travelers. Ty slapped down two nickels, and the boys were soon across the Saginaw River, feet planted on the West Side. Electric trolleys, the first anywhere in Michigan, hummed through that side of Bay City and ran every twelve minutes on weekdays and every five on weekends. They jumped on the No. 14 and rolled north through the French-Canadian neighborhood of Banks, past the Last Chance Bar on the corner of Wilder and Park Drive. There, a father gave his children a handful coins and hopped off the bus for an afternoon at the speakeasy. The trolley continued on, and Stanley leaned out the window, searching through the treetops for the white kiosks and red roofs. In the distance, the buzz of engines purred overhead. Soon the high hill of the Jack Rabbit roller coaster emerged into view, and the Wenona Beach Amusement Park was just around the corner.

When they got off the trolley, Stanley sprinted to the arched gates that opened into a fantastic midway. Willow trees, flower patches, and kissing couples speckled the fairgrounds. The tinny tunes of the calliope sang with shouts of laughter and glee from all directions. People wore their Sunday best: women in their finest dresses, complete with hats and parasols, men in their boots and pressed suits lighting fresh cigars. Concession stands stuffed kids with peanuts and cotton candy. Bowtied barkers directed individuals toward the game booths inside the Midway Arcade. There, men, women, and children alike waved their tokens, vying for a chance to take home stuffed animals or homemade desserts.

For the more adventurous, the Joy Wheel water ride and the Circular Swings spun with great speed to the delight and fear of their riders. Children clutching pennies rushed to secure their places in line for the merry-go-round, the Ferris wheel, and the treacherous climb of the wooden Jack Rabbit roller coaster.

Couples looking for an evening away from the kids spent the night at the Casino. This entertainment hall was famous across Central Michigan and drew actors and comedians like W. C. Fields and the Marx Brothers to Bay City annually. Couples danced as touring bands and musicians whirled and strummed and rattled and pazsazzed. Steaming plates of venison and duck were served to the hungry patrons, and, for that special occasion, the chef's platter of steak and whitefish was available for a steal at only fifty cents. The feasting couples toasted local politicians who had cut a deal with the governor to exempt the Casino every Saturday night from Michigan's wartime prohibition. Mug after mug of brew was ordered up with great liberty as people tried to forget about the uncertainties of the frontline.

Most people were able to lose themselves in the evening's festivities, but in the dark recesses of the music hall, tables of solitary patrons hid. These people tried to enjoy the mingling and merriment but couldn't free themselves from their thoughts. Patrons like Karl Hansel who learned his brother in the 33rd had been shredded by enemy fire after he'd fallen asleep on watch. Or Vern O'Malley who snapped at the waitress for his seventh whiskey because the memory of his slain cousin refused to fade from his mind. Or Henrik and Ana Sinicki, who after more than a week, still hadn't seen their son leave his bedroom.

The Kowalczyk boys breezed past the Casino and the rest of the Promenade to the planked path that led to the most popular area of the park: the beach. Fathers and mothers lounged back on blankets and watched their children build fortresses in the sand. A few brave boys played football in the frigid knee-high water as admiring girls giggled and pointed at the sight.

Stanley and Ty hustled to the far end of the shore where the yacht races usually attracted the crowds, but on this particular day the boats were moored at the docks. An airshow was in full swing, and the spectators stared skyhigh. Stanley saw Henry Dora and Lionel DeRemer and their flying machine, the very plane he admired daily on his route. Three other bi-winged crafts waited in a row. Their single propellers spun in a solid blur, humming eagerly to climb to magnificent heights.

Stanley and Ty found a seat on the sand just as the first flying vehicle started off with a set of passengers. The four airplanes were in constant motion, one landing, one loading and unloading, one taking off, and the fourth streaking across the sky. Stanley couldn't take his eyes off the airborne craft. It spiraled and turned and banked and plummeted, and for the first time, he felt a twinge of fear in his stomach. Not at the thought of flying, but at the realization that there were so many ways his father could be knocked from the sky by a German tri-plane.

"Are you ready?" Ty asked.

Stanley's face glowed in disbelief. "Can we afford it?"

"Five dollars a person?" Ty flashed a ten dollar bill from his pocket. "No problem."

"You too?"

Ty nodded, and Stanley sprinted to the end of the

line, anxiously awaiting his turn. His eyes searched the crowd for the main attraction. Two more planes landed before Stanley spotted him. Clad in his tight leather cap with goggles bulging over his eyes, there stood Orville Wright. Dora and DeRemer had convinced their teacher to join them for the local airshow. Stanley couldn't take his eyes off his hero.

When his turn finally came, Stanley was momentarily disappointed not to be riding in Wright's airplane, but he raced up the steps into the back seat of Dora's craft. He pressed himself against the far side to get a good look over the edge, and Ty slid in beside him. They strapped the belt across their laps as the DH-4 jolted forward, sputtering toward the runway. The pilot checked his instruments and sped down the path. The airplane hopped into the air, hovering for a moment, then bounced back to the earth as it tried to pull itself off the ground. Stanley peered through his tangling hair as the land plummeted beneath him, and the bi-winged plane was soaring through the sky. The smells of burning oil and gasoline mixed with the lake mist and clung to Stanley's lips. He could see the Saginaw River splitting the city in two and the shipyards where Uncle Stash worked. Stanley swore he could even see his house nestled in the South End. He yelled to his brother, but Ty didn't hear a word over the engine. Stanley tugged his sleeve and pointed below. Ty nodded in understanding.

Stanley peered back over the side and absorbed the sights on the ground. All of the new details and stories that would come from this flight. He couldn't wait to get home to fill countless typed pages with the sounds and smells that made this day unforgettable.

2

"No, I don't have any of those tables in stock," Franek snapped.

The couple was offended by the sharp outburst and headed for the door.

"That's right," Franek yelled after them. "Nothing here is worth buying. Nothing!"

He slammed his fist against a bookshelf beside him, and a ceramic figurine toppled and smashed to the floor. If it wasn't the popularity of his nephew's tables, it was the valor of his brother. Franek wouldn't allow himself to be esteemed beneath those two. So he withdrew from the South End society. No poker games. No drinking at Pulaski Hall. Men once considered friends, he rarely, if ever, saw. Franek knew this would only evoke more public rebuke, but for all he had done, those men owed him respect.

The front door rang open, but Franek didn't bother to look at Ty's latest admirer. He swept the ceramic shards into a pile with his foot. Someone called out to him, and Franek turned. Andrzej stood in the doorway, his frame frazzled and worn but markedly distinguished. Franek restrained his unexpected relief at the sight of his brother. He didn't want to seem too excited at his return. Franek nodded to Andrzej and turned back to the mess. "It's good that you're home," he said over his shoulder.

Andrzej walked toward him. The men shook hands and embraced awkwardly. Franek stepped away.

"You must help me," Andrzej said.

Already he orders me around, Franek thought. "What?"

"I need money. To pay someone back."

"One of your fellow soldiers?"

Andrzej shrugged. "I do not want to say."

How he pretends to be modest, Franek thought, bragging about his mission. "I can't give you money," he said curtly. "Things here are different."

"Different? What do you mean?"

"Haven't you seen your family?"

"No, you are the first person I have seen. Are they all right?"

"They're fine. But your business isn't doing well."

"What is wrong? Is it losing money?"

"Money isn't the problem, Andrzej. But you should hear the talk around town."

"Who talks? What do they say?"

"Nothing that bad, yet. But many people wonder how things will be once you return."

"What things?"

"Ty and Tekla don't sell me tables anymore."

"What?"

"Stash helps them go door to door. I'll admit, they make a little more money for each table, but the way people are talking. 'Kowalczyk's wife and boy run his business.' 'They won't need him when he returns.'"

"Who says that?"

Franek shrugged. "The men at Pulaski's. I try to defend you, but what can I say when my own family won't sell to me."

"How long has this gone on?"

"For some time. There's even some talk about how unreliable your business is. Ty let a few sales slip through his fingers."

"I can not afford that." Andrzej's voice tinged with

anger.

"I warned him, but he thinks he knows more. He says he runs your business better. I tried to reason with him, but he's stubborn. I was hoping you'd return home before I moved on but—"

"What do you mean, move on?"

"To find a new tablemaker."

"Do not Franek."

"Two carpenters have already made me an offer."

"I will sell to you again. I will change things back."

"I've already met with them."

"Give me a chance. I am home now."

Franek leaned back against his desk, pretending to consider this. "Perhaps a couple of days. That's the best I can give you."

"Do not worry. I will straighten everything."

"If you do, I'll even give you four extra dollars for each table."

"Four extra dollars? That would be great. Same number each week?"

"Yes. And plenty of Ty's tables too."

"Ty's tables? Why?"

"He carves beautiful furniture, like nothing you've ever made. But I know you taught him everything he knows," Franek chuckled.

Andrzej's eyebrows rose. "Yes, I did."

A smile glided across Franek's face. "I'm glad you're home, Andrzej. We are brothers and we must help each other, yes?"

"Yes." Andrzej clasped Franek's hand firmly. "We must."

"Let me know tomorrow."

"I will." Andrzej looked his brother in the eye. "Franek, can I get that advance now?"

"When you get me some of Ty's tables, I'll help you."

3

The foreman roared at the field hands for their idleness, and the workers darted their heads down, rushing through the motions of digging in the dirt. Their boss snorted at their effort and stormed away up the row. Once he was far enough away yelling at a different group, the workers dove back into their heated, whispered debate.

"I heard he took over one-thousand dollars."

Another harvester shook his head. "Erasmo says it was a bag of rare silver coins."

"No, no, no," a third man countered. "The deed to his family's estate was stolen and is being held for money."

No one was supposed to know about the robbery, but rumors spread like weeds across the fields. The only fact that everyone knew for certain was that the thief had left a note. A simple, taunting note.

I will pay you back as soon as I can.

Even more insulting, the bandit had boldly signed his name.

The morning after the robbery, the foreman had forbidden anyone from mentioning the man's name again, and any worker who did was fired on the spot. Three men had already suffered that fate. The field hands felt the greatest, albeit secret, pride and respect for their fellow worker's defiance. They retold the story over and over, referring to the man in the native language of the area: *el bandido*.

A few days later, the foreman overheard a group of field hands laughing about Tavo's late night visitor. The men were immediately thrown off the property. That night, charged with whiskey in his blood, the foreman barged into Tavo's casino and demanded his money.

Tavo laughed in his face.

The foreman drew a pistol, but Tavo's bouncers were quick with their own guns and knives. The foreman begrudgingly put his weapon away. "That's my money," he spat.

"What are you talking about?" Tavo asked with a challenging smile.

"You know. The money you got the other night."

"Are you calling me a liar?"

The foreman started to respond, then reconsidered.

Tavo stood up from his chair and stepped toward the foreman. His voice hardened. "Are you?"

He held Tavo's eyes. "No."

"Because if you are—"

"No. You're not lying."

Tavo circled the foreman. "Let me give you some advice. I am respected because I earn respect. When people owe me money, they pay me back, no matter how late at night." A few muffled laughs rose from the back of the casino, and the foreman clenched his teeth. "Obviously," Tavo continued, "*el bandido* doesn't fear you or your word. If you let this man steal from you, soon all men will steal from you."

The foreman stared down the insult.

Tavo closed in on the foreman's face and hissed. "But I don't think you can catch him." Tavo turned to the men in his casino and called out, "Does anybody?"

A chorus of taunts answered back.

The foreman bolted out of the casino, trying to maintain a scrap of dignity. He banged on his supervisors' barrack and ordered the five men, who were groggy with slumber and booze, to his office.

"Come on, Dolton," the foreman's younger brother objected, "they say he's from Michigan."

"How will we find him there?" another supervisor added.

"That'll cost more than he stole," the brother complained, yawning. "Just let him go."

The foreman grabbed his brother by the collar and slammed him against the wall. "If you want your part of the inheritance, you'll find him!"

4

Ty had been sleeping in fits and spurts. Ten minutes here, thirty minutes there, at any point in the day, but rarely at night. Sometimes he'd shut his eyes just as the sun rose above the horizon. Or at midday, right after he was supposed to eat lunch. Or one afternoon when he climbed into the loft to get some lumber and fell asleep leaning against the stack of boards.

Today, Ty sprang awake from his slouched position at the workbench when the barn door slammed shut. He lifted his head and glanced over his shoulder. He thought he was still asleep, suspended in a dream.

"Father?"

He rubbed his eyes and saw the figure walking toward him. "Father!" Ty leapt to his feet and dashed toward the door, arms spread wide to embrace. His father held out his hand and motioned Ty to calm down. He restrained himself to an uncontrollable grin and shook his father's hand. "It's great to have you home, father. How was the war?"

"I do not want to talk about it."

Ty sprinted toward the barn door. "I'll get mother."

"Wait! I want to talk to you first."

Ty stopped and turned back.

"What have you done to my business?" his father asked.

Ty grinned. "Have you heard the great news?"

His father's face hardened. "I saw Franek, and he told me you do not sell tables to him anymore. Is that true?"

"Yes."

"Your uncle and I had an agreement for years."

"We're making more money selling them on our own."

"That is not the way I run my business."

"But we're more successful. I work all day, and Stanley helps out after his homework."

"His homework?"

"Yes, father. He's back in school."

"How is that possible? We needed all three of us to finish the tables before."

"Mother helps too."

"Your mother works in my barn?"

"She does everything. She even carves."

"What do the neighbors think?"

"Nothing," Ty said confused.

"Never once in fifteen years has your mother worked a day in this barn. It is my job to provide the money. *My* job. You do not see Sawicki's wife in his shop. Linkowski's wife does not work in his stable. Andrzej Kowalczyk's wife will not either."

"We needed to get the work done."

"All at my expense. It is true what Franek says. People talk about me and my business, call me a gypsy."

"Nobody talks bad about you, father. People admire your business. Last week we received over forty orders."

"Forty orders?"

"Yes."

His father calculated this in his head. "That is hundreds of dollars. Ty, is that true?"

He nodded.

"How long will it take to finish those and get them to Franek?"

"Those customers ordered from us. We don't need Uncle Franek."

"He will give me four dollars more for each."

"Four dollars more?"

"And he promised me an advance."

"We don't need an advance. Look at what I make."

Ty led his father past the taunting piles of untouched pieces to the three tables against the side wall that were in various stages of completion. His father knelt before them, amazed at the craftsmanship. He ran his hand across the stained finish.

"You made these yourself?"

"Yes." Ty glowed with pride and handed his father a sculpted leg. "It takes a couple days to carve the pieces."

Intricate grooves and ridges stretched the length of the piece. "How did you learn this?" his father asked.

"I practice with mother every night."

"With mother?"

"Yes." Ty took the leg from his father. "People tell other people about my work, and now customers ask me to build them bureaus and desks."

His father stood up. "We do not make those things here. We build tables, and nothing else."

"But look at the opportunity. For all these years, Uncle Franek only let you make tables, but we can make anything people need."

"How much do you charge?"

"That is the best. We charge the same as Uncle Franek. We keep a larger amount and the customers get a great deal. We make over twelve dollars."

"Over twelve dollars?" His father's eyes widened. "That is great. How much money have you collected?"

"Only enough to purchase the lumber and supplies for each order. They pay the rest on delivery."

"I need money quickly."

"For what?"

His father picked up a different carved piece from

the workbench. "To help a fellow I met."

"One of your soldier friends?" Ty exclaimed.

His father hesitated, his eyes fixed on the wooden panel in his hand. "I do not want to say."

"Was he a part of your battalion?"

"I do not want to talk about it."

Ty leaned back from his father's tone.

"Is it true that others disrespect me?" his father asked.

"Did Uncle Franek tell you that?"

"Yes."

"He only says that to get these orders. People admire your business."

"I have worked with Franek for so long. He is family."

"When did he ever get you forty orders?"

His father shrugged.

"We can start collecting as soon as I finish these," Ty added. "I'll keep working from sunrise to midnight. And with Stanley and mother helping—"

"Your mother will not work in here anymore."

"But—"

"Not in my barn. Not anymore. And Stanley will quit school."

"I was getting everything done with their help. And now with you home, we can work twice as fast. Stanley can stay in school."

His father pressed his lips together. "Fine. I will allow that. But if you can not finish the work as you say, he will come out of school for good. No wasting time, no—"

"I won't, father. I promise. I won't let you down."

5

Kowalczyk stepped in front of his bedroom mirror and took a deep breath. For the entire trip across the country, he had pushed the thoughts from his mind, but now his stomach quivered. Ty had sprinted to get Tekla from work. How would Andrzej explain to her why he hadn't returned.

Andrzej heard the door swing open and slam shut, then footsteps raced up the hallway. Ty popped his head in through the door. "Come quickly. Mother's on her way." He disappeared.

Kowalczyk looked around for someplace to hide, someplace to escape. But there was nothing he could do to stop this. He walked down the hallway, through the living room, and into the kitchen. A stampede of people hustled up the back porch into his house. Chester Neizwicki. Barton and Ionia Sczapanski. Rupert Grozczek. William and Rebeka Trovclov. Avery Hryniewicz. Andrzej tried to retreat to the living room, but the group attacked him. Dorota Kaczynski kissed his cheeks. Piotr Wojek patted his back. Sonja Gudzinowicz tousled his hair. Hands grabbed him and pulled in different directions. Bodies pressed against his. Voices chattered in English and Polish, and Andrzej couldn't understand a word. And the hands kept reaching.

"Stop it!"

An awkward silence engulfed the room. Andrzej's feverish eyes darted from person to person. He backed away. The door slammed shut, and Tekla emerged from the front of the crowd. Andrzej saw her and clung to his wife like a small child, burying his head into her shoulder.

"I just want to be alone," he muttered. "Alone."

Tekla led him to the bedroom and eased him into a chair. Then she closed the door and returned to the kitchen. The calmed crowd asked what was wrong, and Tekla ensured them that everything was all right and that as soon as Andrzej rested, they'd invite everyone over.

Later that night, Andrzej wrapped himself in his bed, eyes fixed forward, trying to comprehend the rush of visitors.

The closed door peeked open, and Stanley nudged his head into the room.

"Can I come in?"

Andrzej didn't look toward the door but nodded. His son crept inside and pulled a chair bedside and sat down. His face was blank with uncertainty.

Andrzej whispered, almost begging for an answer. "Why do so many people come over?"

Stanley's face lit up, eyes wide with pride. "Because, father, you're a hero."

"A hero?" Andrzej's brow furrowed. "Why do you say that?"

Stanley leaned forward. "Your secret mission in France. Everyone knows you're not allowed to talk about it, but they want to hear whatever details you can tell."

Andrzej couldn't believe what he heard.

"I've flown too, father." Stanley smiled proudly.

Kowalczyk stared off into the floor. "Let me rest."

His son nodded eagerly. "We can talk later."

Andrzej felt he needed to respond so he closed his

eyes. He heard Stanley slide the chair back as quietly as he could, tiptoe out of the room, and close the door.

Kowalczyk opened his eyes.

He had always hoped, always dreamed of returning home a hero, and now it was apparently true. Where did they get such thoughts? This dream was more unsettling than he ever imagined.

With that, Andrzej locked himself in the permanent darkness of his shade-drawn bedroom for the rest of the week, refusing to see anyone. Whenever visitors stopped by, he claimed to be too tired or not ready to meet people. The guests were disappointed but accepted this and left their plates of paczki and pierogis, and their bottles of vodka and miód pitny for the returned hero.

Most challenging for Kowalczyk were his own sons. An hour didn't pass without Ty asking him to go down to Pulaski Hall for a toast. Or Stanley, who was always two steps behind him, bombarding him with questions about the war and his experience in France and MacArthur's 42nd Division and corned beef and Sopwith Camel bi-planes and kite balloons and American flying ace Eddie Rickenbacker and Gatling guns and petrol fumes and. . . .

It was too much for Andrzej to digest.

6

With his father back, Ty became a fury of creativity and carving. He attacked the forty-two orders that only days before had seemed insurmountable. It wasn't just having his father home, but the fact he had sided with his business decision over Uncle Franek's. Ty would prove to his father he made the right choice.

Hours and days flew by as he tore through the piles of untouched pieces at a relentless pace. Six legs in the morning, three side panels that afternoon, two shelves in the evening. Ty would finish a leg and hand it to his father who would hold the piece with his eyes so preciously, so appreciatively, turning it over, inspecting its every cove and contour. Then, he would cradle it back to Ty, as if he didn't know what to do with it, as if he wasn't worthy of holding it. Ty chuckled at his father's exaggerated reaction.

Ty even offered to show him how to carve and gave him a leg to practice on. But his father shook his head and said he wasn't interested in learning something new. He was going to build tables the way he always had. Simple, basic tables.

Ty respected that for now. He knew that once his father recovered from his wartime jitters, he would be eager to learn how to carve.

The stories of Andrzej's return home hit the Polish

weekly newspaper, the *Sztandar*. Some of the men at Pulaski's read about their local hero with much anticipation and pride. The *Sztandar* promised exclusive stories over the next couple weeks, starting with interviews with his close friends Sal Krymski and Josef Sczesniak. That is strange, Andrzej thought as he read the article, those men never paid me any attention before. There were other men like Jan Zubek who couldn't stand the articles about Andrzej Kowalczyk. Envy festered inside their chests and mouths, and every word they uttered about Andrzej reeked of insult and jealousy. And they had never even met him. But the majority of the Polish families reacted as most did to local highlights. With complete indifference. They read the articles, nodded their heads with momentary interest, and then turned the page and forgot about the whole thing.

The rest of Bay City knew nothing about Andrzej Kowalczyk. Outside of the South End no one bothered with the *Sztandar* or its news. For days after his father returned home, Stanley waited outside the *Times-Tribune* office before school, hoping to catch a reporter. On Wednesday morning he met one, and Stanley was so excited that he sped through the stories of his father's exploits. The reporter couldn't understand a single word he said. He patted Stanley on the head and told him to head out on his deliveries.

With the number of people constantly knocking on his door, Andrzej felt that every person in every neighborhood of Bay City knew about his heroics. He wanted to rush down to Pulaski's or to the *Sztandar* and admit that none of it was true. He had nothing to do with it. Someone else had created those rumors. He was just a regular, normal person.

But did he really want to continue being that type of person?

Kowalczyk couldn't deny he was partially captivated

by the circulating rumors. He imagined walking through the streets and being respected. More than anything, Andrzej wanted to preserve that look on Franek's face when he had first stepped into his store. In that moment, there was a flash of awe in his brother's eyes. Kowalczyk was certain of it. For the entire time he had been home, his brother was the only person who hadn't questioned him about his war experience or even come by to see him. Perhaps there was a hint of jealousy in his brother's disinterest, Kowalczyk thought. Perhaps being a hero was not such a bad idea—

"Where were you, Andrzej?"

Tekla's voice tore him away from his thoughts. "What?"

"Where were you stationed?" his wife asked as she slid into bed beside him.

Kowalczyk felt his stomach tighten. "I do not want to talk about it." He refused to look her in the eye.

"Was it that horrible?" She waited for an answer. He said nothing. "The stories the men discuss," she continued, "they try to talk when I'm not around, but I hear. They say you switched battalions and—"

"I do not want to talk about it."

The light from the bedside lamp glowed on them.

"Ty has been selling much," Tekla said, breaking the silence. "More than I ever imagined."

"That is good. I need money."

"For what?"

Andrzej cursed himself for broaching the topic. "I have to pay someone back."

"Who?"

"A man."

"From your battalion?"

Andrzej stared up at the ceiling. He felt uncomfortable lying to his wife, but the word *yes* flowed so easily from his lips. It didn't sound false or trembling as he suspected. It was almost too easy.

"For what?"

"It is difficult to explain."

"I'll understand."

Andrzej sighed. "It is late, Tekla. I need to sleep." He turned the lamp off and settled into his pillow, knowing he wasn't tired. His eyes wandered in the distance as he realized this was only the first of many interrogations he would endure from his wife, his sons, the rest of the South End.

"When do you have to pay him back?" Tekla's voice asked.

He snapped his eyelids shut and froze, like a small child feigning sleep.

"Andrzej," she whispered.

He held his position, ten seconds, thirty, a full minute, until it seemed long enough to roll over on his side, his back to his wife, just as he imagined a person in deep slumber would do.

His eyelids floated open, and he wondered how long he could avoid answering questions.

7

Andrzej stood alone in the barn paralyzed. He had built tables for over thirty years, and now he didn't know where to begin, or even how. Naturally, he had grown rusty with his months away, but that wasn't the problem. All of the finely crafted tables surrounding him, how could he possibly produce anything of that quality?

The front door squeaked open. His brother Franek stepped inside, and Andrzej's stomach twittered with unease.

"It's been five days. Why haven't you gotten back to me?"

"I was tired, Franek."

"The new war hero too tired even for his own brother."

Kowalczyk shrugged apologetically.

Franek pulled order forms from his pocket. "I need two tables by Friday. And three more by next week for people on Center."

Andrzej mumbled in response.

Franek stepped over to the side wall, admiring the finished tables stacked there. "What did you say?"

Andrzej couldn't look his brother in the eye. "We are not selling tables to you."

Franek turned around. "What do you mean?"

"Ty explained how—"

"Ty explained to you?" Franek repeated incredulously. "What kind of owner are you, letting an inexperienced boy run your business? His success is beginner's luck."

"Many people want our tables. You just said so."

Franek waved the order forms in his hand. "These are *my* customers. They are interested in buying products from me. They have seen your work Andrzej and bought your furniture only as a favor to me. Ty's surge won't last."

"We have over forty orders."

"I know how many orders you have," Franek snapped.

"Ty says—"

"I don't care what Ty says. Do you know how the men at Pulaski will react to this? You'll be the laughing stock. The man whose boy runs his business. How will you show your face to them?"

"They respect me." Andrzej's eyes were fixed on the ground.

"They don't. They respect Ty and his work."

Andrzej grimaced.

"Three furniture makers from Saginaw begged to work with me when you left," Franek pushed harder, "but I told them no. Family is more important to me than a few extra dollars. Even when other tablemakers called your work unskilled, I told them my brother had talent. I kept my end of the agreement, but you dismiss it."

"I know but—"

"I paid you when no one else considered you. And this is how you repay me. Relying on me during the tough times, turning your back during the good."

Guilt swelled in Kowalczyk's gut.

"The money you need to borrow," Franek continued, "forget it. That will go to my new carpenter."

"Perhaps we could split the tables," Andrzej blurted out. "You can carry some, and we can sell some on our own."

"Don't pity me."

"It is not pity, Franek. You are right. We should work together. I can give you one table a week. Maybe two."

"That's just like you to taunt me. To flaunt your success in my face and abandon me."

"What can I give you, Franek?"

"Your word. That is what I want."

Andrzej hesitated.

"You're a disgrace, treating me this way." Franek walked toward the door.

"Wait. Tell me what to do?"

Franek turned and faced Andrzej. "Meet the orders I have. Five tables. Two by Friday. The rest by next week."

"That is so many."

"See, your words are empty."

"All right, I will give you five tables."

"By the time I ask? Give me your word."

"Yes, you have my word."

"And other tables, whenever I need orders filled?"

Andrzej sighed, realizing the weight of the request. He rubbed his forehead in thought.

"Well?" his older brother demanded.

"No, Uncle Franek," Ty stepped in from the barn threshold, "we won't give you that. Father, don't let him cheat you."

"Is this how you let your son talk to you? To me?" Franek charged Andrzej. "Tell him of our agreement that he will follow."

Andrzej stood there, torn between his brother and son, unwilling to make his own decision. He grimaced and looked toward his son. "I told him we would fill his five orders." He squirmed under Ty's stare. "I gave him my word."

"What else have you promised him?"

Franek objected. "Andrzej you said—"

"What else?" Ty demanded.

"Nothing else." Andrzej's eyes drifted to the floor.

"Fine." Ty turned to his uncle. "I will make the five tables you were promised. But that is all."

"Andrzej, you said both of us would sell them. You said."

"Ty," Andrzej pleaded with his son, "we are all family. We should help each other sell tables."

Ty folded his arms across his chest. "Here's what we can do. I will make the tables to fill our orders here. Father, you can make tables for him."

"That isn't fair," Franek protested.

"Why?" Ty said. "We both have tables."

"I need some of yours."

"I will build the five you were promised. You have my father's word."

Franek and Ty stared each other down.

"Franek," Andrzej offered, "that is good, yes? Everyone is happy."

"That isn't fair."

"Don't you want my father's tables?" Ty asked.

Franek glared at his nephew.

"I can produce two, maybe three a week," Andrzej assured his brother. "That should be good."

"Well?" Ty insisted.

"Fine, I will take your tables," Franek spat.

"For four dollars more, as you promised?"

A scowl crinkled Franek's lips. "Yes, for four dollars more."

"And you will give father the advance you promised him after you receive the tables."

Franek glared at his nephew.

"That was his word, right, father?"

"Yes."

"Fine," Franek relented.

"Good, now we are all helping each other," Ty said. "If you don't mind, Uncle Franek, we have orders to finish."

8

A truck driver may remember Lulu's Pie Stand off the highway entering Oklahoma, or the coffee and biscuits at Lawton's Grille in South Bend, Indiana, or the steak and potatoes at Mickey's Saloon in Sheboygan, Wisconsin, but most of his transcontinental journeys are a collection of streaks and smears and blurs. Towns and cities blend together in a swirl of Main Streets and barber shop poles. This smudge of landscape compounds the loneliness of the long hauls, and most truckers are eager to pick up hitchhikers to break the solitude. Even if the drive passes in complete silence, sharing the space in the cab is a relief.

But for Beaumont Crane, these conversations with wayward travelers were what he craved. This gray haired, fifty-year-old roadman found a natural bond with wanderers. One that few others understood, or cared to have. The anonymity between complete strangers and the certainty of never seeing each other again allowed each person to reach a comfortable level of openness. They were free from the stigma of professed dreams. Just being around Beaumont Crane gave people a sense of safety and ease that inspired them to share their lifelong burdens. He rarely spoke more than a dozen words before his passengers poured out their most guarded moments. He listened intensely and stored away the details, not to wallow in their desperate pity or to gloat over other's misfortunes, but to keep a memorial to their remarkable lives, no matter how joyous or anguished.

When people left Beaumont Crane's cab, most felt as if they had gained a close friend, even though they hadn't asked the driver a single question about his life.

Beaumont Crane wasn't surprised that afternoon on his layover in Austin when five men approached him and asked if he recognized their friend.

"Blackish hair?" Beaumont inquired.

"Yeah," said the foreman's brother.

"Talkèd a lot about Ty Cobb and the Tigers?"

"That's the guy."

"I picked him up in McAllen last week and took him all the way to Dallas."

"Really?" The men exchanged looks. The foreman's brother continued, "You see, we work with him, and he had an emergency back home. His family's house burned down, and we wanted to help. The thing is, he left in such a rush, we weren't able to learn what city in Michigan."

Beaumont scratched his chin. "He said something about a lumbertown in central Michigan. Along the coast somewhere, but I don't remember exactly. He kept talking about his brother and being in the war and how—"

"Coast of central Michigan?" the brother interrupted.

"Yep."

"Thanks, buddy. That helps us out."

———

People kept arriving at Kowalczyk's house, wanting to hear his stories from the warfront. From the confines of his bedroom, Andrzej mumbled to his wife and sons that he wasn't up for talking or was too exhausted or had too much to do or a dozen other excuses why he couldn't see them. The visitors worried more and more about Kowalczyk's seclusion, and Andrzej knew they'd be back in a couple days to check on him again. He would be ready with new excuses.

After a week, Kowalczyk grew tired of his bedroom and forced himself to work inside the barn all hours of the day. Or, to be more accurate, he spent time moving around from area to area, giving the impression of work and activity when he did little more than watch Ty finish orders. Anything to keep himself from having to interact with visitors. Andrzej passed his time by keeping mental totals of each sale, convinced he would soon have enough money to repay the foreman.

Occasionally, Kowalczyk grabbed one of Ty's carved pieces to sand and became more impressed, and more intimidated, by his son's ability. Andrzej had never seen such carpentry skills in the thirty years he worked. He couldn't bring himself to even think about building a table in that type of environment. And the way Tekla continued to spend her evenings working in the barn. He couldn't believe her defiance of his order.

One morning after Andrzej spent thirty minutes stirring a can of stain, Ty approached him and offered him a handful of bills. Kowalczyk looked up confused.

"There's a card game this afternoon," Ty explained. "You should go."

Andrzej's body tightened with fear. "We have much work to do and—"

"You're caught up. I'll carve more for you to sand tomorrow."

"It is not right to leave you with all the work."

His son looked him in the eye. "Father, the men at Pulaski's look up to you. They want to see you. Why don't you want to go?"

Andrzej opened his mouth to respond but stopped. He simply shook his head, then mixed the stain.

The next day his son urged him to try carving. Andrzej didn't want to, but it was better than having to play poker at Pulaski's.

Ty handed him a piece of wood and a knife. "Carve what you see. Bring the piece inside to life."

Andrzej didn't exactly understand what his son meant, but he didn't need to be told what to do. He knew the intricacies of wood as any woodsmith did. He sliced into the block and whittled it down. He made sure to keep the top squared off and worked down the flue, honing it at its base.

"That's a good start," Ty encouraged him. "Like the curves of a vase or the calf of your leg."

Andrzej didn't see what those things had to do with wood, but as he carved, the sides of the leg never turned out symmetrical. Either one sloped too much or the descent of one side started higher than the other. Andrzej spent the entire afternoon adding to the scrap bin. In the same amount of time, Ty finished four legs of remarkable design. Kowalczyk rose from the bench and headed for the door.

"It takes time," Ty said. "Don't let it bother you."

Andrzej could hear only condescension in his son's voice. He mumbled a response and slunk out into the clearing, away from the sawdust and failure.

A voice shouted his name. Kowalczyk saw Avery Hryniewicz walking up the path. "Come for drinks and poker," he called. "Already Matuszewski and Cianek are waiting."

His throat tightened, and Kowalczyk shook his head. "I am just taking a small break. There is much work to do. Another night."

Hryniewicz sighed.

"Do not worry, Avery," Andrzej assured him, retreating to the barn. "I will join you soon. I just need some time to get my feet under me."

Andrzej closed the barn door behind him. Ty continued to carve and didn't notice his return. Kowalczyk plodded to the back corner of the work area, grabbed a piece of coarse wood, and sanded it, a job set aside for his youngest son.

This routine continued for days, adding to Andrzej's frustration, trapped between incompetence in the barn and questions at Pulaski Hall. Andrzej found the only place he could escape was at the back of his lot amidst a cluster of pine trees. There, he draped himself in the solitude of the timber.

One afternoon, after contributing sufficiently to the scrap bin, Andrzej saw Stanley march out toward him and plop down beside him on the fallen trunk.

"Miss Noonan gave me a perfect score on my story today," he claimed with a smile.

"That is good," Andrzej muttered flatly.

"She especially liked my description of petrol fuel and bloodshot eyes."

Kowalczyk nodded.

"Did you like flying, father?"

Andrzej shrank from the question. "I never flew, Stanley."

"You didn't?" his son gasped, as if it was the most inconceivable statement ever made.

"No, I did not."

"You were in France, right?" Stanley asked.

His voice squirmed. "I do not want to talk about it, Stanislaw."

"You never want to talk," his son persisted. "Were the fields caked with mud and oil as the papers say?"

"It is not the thing to talk about with a child."

"Miss Noonan's fiancé flies a Sopwith Camel for the Regiment. He wrote to her about the peasants in a French village and how they cheered and clapped for the American soldiers. Did people do that for you?"

"Nobody noticed us that way."

"Did you eat poached eggs and brandy and milk?"

"How do you know all this?"

"Miss Noonan reads us letters and articles."

"Really?"

Stanley nodded.

"And you remember it all?"

"I use the details in my stories. That's how I do so well with my grades."

"What else does she tell you?"

Stanley explained to his father about the bi-wing fighters and the French tanks in the Argonne Forest and the British Calvary and the German U-boats and the canvas wings of the DH-4s and the dogfights with the Red Baron and the doughboys and the push into St. Mihiel and the Americans in Belleau Woods and . . . .

9

Kowalczyk's unwillingness to meet with people, to talk to them, to even say hello intensified the already horrific images believed by the people in the South End. Rumors circulated uncontrollably. Wiktoria Klinski claimed Andrzej had torched soldiers with a flame thrower. Eugene Stolczyk was certain he had led an attack using mustard gas against Kaiser's troops. Herbert Rupanski's cousin insisted Andrzej was the lone survivor of a massacred battalion.

At Wilson's, workers bombarded Tekla with questions, looking for any information she could share.

"He refuses to talk about his location," she said to Edith Czapla.

"Andrzej won't say anything about his mission," she explained to Lottie Sawicki.

"He hasn't mentioned a word of his battalion," she snapped at Eleanor Linkowski.

"He doesn't tell me anything," she lashed out at her supervisor in front of six workers.

That was when she knew it was too much not to know about her own husband. She asked to be left alone for the rest of the shift, and everyone respected her space.

When her shift was over, Tekla found her brother waiting outside the plant.

"Good evening, Stash."

He nodded hello as he always did, and they walked together in silence down Farragut Street. They covered four blocks before Stash spoke. "Andrzej keeps urging

Ty to build faster to make more money."

"He talks of that often."

"To pay back someone from the war?"

"That's what he says."

"Tekla, you know I'll help you in any way."

She stopped and faced her brother. "I know, Stash, but promise me, you won't give Andrzej any money until I say it's all right."

"I don't understand."

"Promise me," she insisted.

"Yes, I promise."

They passed another block in silence as the threat of snow whispered in the crunch of grass beneath their steps.

Stash cleared his throat. "Why can't I help now?"

"I know Andrzej is lying about this money. Until he explains the whole story, I won't let you help him."

"Why do you think he needs it?"

"I don't know, Stash. He refuses to tell me anything."

In three days Ty finished not only the five tables for his uncle but also three of the Thanksgiving Day orders. He was keeping pace with Uncle Stash's cutting and the piles of uncarved pieces were beginning to dwindle. Ty noticed his father moving around the barn but not really helping with any of the building. He wouldn't even hammer finished pieces together, fearing he would split the wood.

That was what Ty had been thinking when he drifted off to sleep Friday afternoon. He had taken a short break to grab an extra wool sweater to fight the chill of the frigid nights and sat down on his bed to rest his eyes for a moment. Then exhaustion overtook him.

The long nights carving in front of the fire. Days

building in the barn. Missing meal after meal. Pushing his body beyond its endurance. Hours blended together, and Ty couldn't remember what it was like before he ran his father's business, before tables consumed his every waking moment. But he was making progress on the forty-two orders and felt good—

"Why are you sleeping?"

Ty sprung awake as his father stared down at him.

"You are growing lazy, sleeping your days away. We have money to make. Get up."

"Yes, yes," Ty said as he pulled the wool sweater over his head and raced up the hallway.

His father yelled after him. "I should have stuck with Franek. He never slept at work."

"I'm sorry father. It won't happen again."

The talk of Andrzej's participation in the great defeat of German soldiers on August 8 continued to spread in epic proportions, and Franek couldn't stand a single moment of it. His brother was an inferior man striving to be better, Franek thought, and now he was succeeding. Franek did feel a small bit of pride for Andrzej's accomplishments, but he buried those feelings just like the memories of Cuba. Standing on the shore, petrified as the gunfire zipped past him. He vaguely remembered Tomaz screaming something before shoving him out of the way. By the time Franek lifted himself from the ground, four bullets had torn into Tomaz's chest. Franek came home a celebrated hero even though he couldn't will himself to move through his cowardly paralysis. He had carried the weight of his brother's death for decades. Now he was joined by another Kowalczyk war hero. But this time, Andrzej brought genuine honor to the family name.

The front door rang open, and Franek saw his brother saunter in. "Your tables are ready."

Franek tightened his jaw.

"I left them out back," Andrzej said.

Franek grabbed the keys from his desk and walked to the back door. Without a word the two brothers carried the pieces into the display room, then Franek returned to his desk, busying himself with unnecessary paperwork. Andrzej stepped beside him.

"What?" Franek snapped without looking up.

"I wanted to get the money. Like you said."

How he gloats, Franek thought. He leaned back and begrudgingly pulled money from his pocket, counting out the amount for the tables.

Andrzej picked it up. "And the advance?"

Franek's eyes darted up.

"The advance you prom—"

"I know what you mean. I won't give it to you."

"You gave your word."

"This is the thanks I get? Five quality tables and you expect an advance."

"I'll deliver the other tables next week."

"I don't want your tables."

"I thought—"

"I have countless orders for Ty's work. Your tables are worthless."

"But Franek, you said—"

Franek bolted to his feet. He wanted to yell, wanted to say something, but he stopped. He knew his words no longer had influence over Andrzej. He was completely powerless. Andrzej stood there, staring, and then, as if to confirm Franek's thoughts, his brother turned and walked out of the store without an apology or compromise. Franek knew it would only be a matter of time before his brother gained complete acceptance in the South End community.

"We should work on orders," he insisted to Ty.

His son didn't break stride. "They've waited almost two weeks to see you. We'll have one drink."

"We can go tomorrow, I promise."

Ty said nothing and continued walking. Kowalczyk followed. When they reached the Hall, his son opened the door and ushered Andrzej inside. Scores of men filled the tables and barstools, sharing the jokes and insults that were common conversation in Pulaski Hall. Isaak Grekowicz and Stefan Brozewski played the fiddle and accordion on stage as a few drunken men danced.

Andrzej surveyed the large room and saw Benya Owsiak stop mid-sentence and notice him. He whispered to Yuri Cianek and Cliff Zwaska beside him. Both men turned. Fingers pointed. Looks spread across the room until not a single voice spoke. Every eye stared at Andrzej.

The heat of self-consciousness rushed up from Kowalczyk's chest into his throat as he tried to endure the silent gaze of the room.

From the back of the hall, two hands met in a crisp, clear clap. They were joined by another set of hands. Then another, until a crescendo of applause filled the room. Shouts and yells welcomed Andrzej home. Igor Tvardek and Avery Hryniewicz embraced him. Hank Sawicki patted him on the back. Manny Kreska ordered two glasses of the hall's best vodka, and every man, young and old, followed his lead, waving for his own drink to toast the returning hero. Men like Sal Krymski and Josef Sczesniak, who had never given Kowalczyk the time of day, were shoved out of the way by others trying to greet him.

A hand yanked Andrzej's arm and dragged him toward the front of Pulaski Hall. It was his son leading him through the crowd, clearing a path to the stage. Andrzej mounted the stairs and took one of the filled glasses Ty offered him. His son raised the other glass above his head, and the voices fell silent. "To my father who has honored us in the fields of France. Now let us honor him here at home."

Cheers rose as glasses clinked, and Ty embraced his father. The fiddle and accordion broke into triumphant songs from the motherland that were saved for the most solemn occasions. All for Andrzej Kowalczyk.

The party raged on, but a group of men led by Jan Zubek refused to participate in the celebration. They gathered their hats and jackets and left the hall. Kowalczyk didn't notice this as countless men surrounded him, struggling to ask him about his war experience. He dismissed these questions with a quick wave of his hand, insisting they would only dampen the spirit of the evening. The men accepted this for the time being and spoke proudly of their own sons and brothers and cousins still fighting with the 33rd. Dziadzia Toporski clasped Andrzej on the back and asked him if he would talk to Ignasiu Sinicki. Andrzej agreed to the request that he only partially heard.

Later in the evening, in the midst of a conversation with Adalbert Ciszek and Jerzy Grabowski, Andrzej caught a glimpse out of the corner of his eye of Ty and Stash lingering against the far wall. Voices faded from Kowalczyk's ears as, he thought, his son grinned at him. Andrzej offered a smile back and raised his glass as a sign of appreciation. Ty didn't acknowledge Andrzej's motion, but his son's intense eyes remained fixed on him. Andrzej tried to return to the conversation with those around him, but he couldn't concentrate. He peeked back in his son's direction, and Ty still stared. A chill shivered up the base of Andrzej's spine as he grew more unnerved with every stolen glance. Kowalczyk knew Stash never liked him. What was he telling his son? He had an odd sensation they were talking about him, doubting him and all of the stories that were circulating. That toast and hug his son had given were only part of an act. I must not let him suspect, Andrzej thought. He tried to smile back again, but his attempt felt transparent, as if confirming his façade. The pats on the back and congratulations continued throughout the night, but Andrzej could only feel his son's disbelieving eyes.

Well past midnight after the music had ended, the remaining men gathered around the bar. Yuri Cianek grabbed a bottle of vodka and filled everyone's glass. "Kowalczyk, it is good to see you out."

"Many worried about you," Avery Hryniewicz said. "No one heard from you for months. It must have been a very difficult mission."

"I should head home," Kowalczyk said, looking for the hat he hadn't brought.

"No, stay," Hank Sawicki insisted.

"You're always at home," Clyde Zwaska complained.

Andrzej muttered, "I know but—"

"Father, stay," Ty said with a tone of respect that offered no other option.

Andrzej held his son's stare for a moment, then sat back down.

"What was it like?" Owsiak asked.

"Yes, Andrzej, what was your mission?" Kreska leaned forward.

"I do not want to talk about it."

"Look how humble our hero is," Cianek joked.

The men laughed and clapped at Kowalczyk's uneasy smile.

"I received a letter from my nephew," Issak

Grekowicz stated. "Jonathan worries he won't make it home."

"So does Steward."

"And my Vladi."

It seemed that every man in the room had a brother or cousin or son in Europe, each name spoken with a voice of prayer and hope.

"What was it like, Andrzej?"

Kowalczyk stared at his wringing hands. "I did not see the 33rd after they left Texas."

"We know," Zwaska said, "but what was Europe like?"

"How were the conditions?"

"Was it really as horrible as the rumors say?" Stefan Brozewski asked.

"Are they treating the men good?"

Kowalczyk looked from face to face, seeing the desperate need these men had. The need to hear information, any information to ease their concern.

"I can not reveal many details," Andrzej said slowly, his eyes fixed on the floor, "because the war lingers. No specific places or events or battalions."

"Yes, yes, Andrzej, we understand."

"Tell us whatever you can."

"Yes, anything you can."

"Where were you?"

Andrzej glanced up and swallowed hard at the eyes fixed on him.

"It is all right, Kowalczyk," Cianek assured him. "We know it is must have been difficult."

"Take your time."

"All I can tell you," he offered, "is that I was in France."

"Really?"

"I would have guessed that," Sawicki claimed.

"What else, Andrzej?"

"Yes, what else?"

"The food," Kowalczyk continued. "We ate poached eggs. And brandy. And milk."

"Was there enough for everyone?"

"Did they ration your meals?"

The men hung on Kowalczyk's every word. It was exhilarating to have their complete attention and respect. He leaned back, a little more calm, enjoying the moment, his hands resting on his knees. "Let me tell you my most memorable day. One afternoon, our battalion reached a peasant village in France and they greeted us with warm welcomes. Cheers and shouts for the Americans and . . . ."

Andrzej continued, weaving stories in about bi-wing fighters and the French tanks in the Argonne Forest and the British Calvary and the German U-boats and dogfights with the Red Baron and. . . .

10

From that day on, Andrzej slipped into the woods behind the barn and waited for Stanley to return home from his paper route. His son shared stories about the war and the soldiers and the lives they endured in Europe. The next day, Andrzej would rush to Pulaski Hall and join the men for their lunchtime card game. He tended to lose a bit here and there, but the money was well-spent. He had an audience.

This went on for more than a week before Andrzej stopped by his brother's store one Wednesday afternoon on his way to the Hall.

"You should come and play."

"I'm busy," Franek stated. "Not everyone can just leave his store."

"One afternoon," Andrzej urged, "that is all I ask."

"No."

Kowalczyk held his position.

"What is it, Andrzej?" Franek snapped.

"You have not stopped by for my celebrations. You have not asked about my experience in Europe, or—"

"Your God damn war experience!" Franek roared. "I have heard enough of it. You are a hero. The greatest in the South End. I know Andrzej. I don't need to hear it again. You and Tomaz were the greatest men of our family. And your business is successful while mine is near bankruptcy. Don't pretend to be shocked. You know full well what you've done to my business. I want you out of here." Franek collapsed into his chair and clenched his forehead.

Kowalczyk stood dumbfounded, staring at his brother.

"You should have—"

"Just leave me alone, Andrzej," Franek growled.

Kowalczyk fidgeted with his hat, then shuffled out of the store into the streets. He started walking toward Pulaski Hall, deep in thought. Andrzej had never seen his brother so crushed and defeated. Slowly, a proud smile eased across his face.

11

When he first borrowed the money in Texas, Andrzej Kowalczyk intended to pay it back, every last cent, but now his thoughts rarely returned to the cantina or the fields. The foreman's loan was a vague memory. Now Andrzej lived lavishly as a hero should. Playing cards. Drinking with the men.

On Sunday afternoon before he headed to gamble, Kowalczyk counted the money he kept in his dresser drawer. There was significantly less than the last time he checked. I could not have lost that much playing cards, he thought. He called out to Tekla, who stepped in from the living room.

"Have you taken any of this money."

"No, Andrzej," she said curtly, "I haven't touched your money."

Kowalczyk started counting the bills again.

"When do you plan to pay that back?" Tekla asked.

"When I have enough."

Tekla sat down on the bed. "Why is that money so important?"

"I have told you many times."

"You haven't told me anything. Where were you stationed?"

"In Europe, as I said."

"No, where were you really?"

"I told you as much as I can."

"Andrzej, they sent me letters. They wanted to know where you were."

Andrzej froze, his eyes fixed on the money before him. "What do you mean?" he asked without turning.

"Men from the military post in Detroit came here. They said you were supposed to be in South Carolina, but you never arrived. They wanted to know if I'd heard from you, Andrzej. Where were you?"

Kowalczyk dashed toward her. "Who knows about this?"

"What?"

He grabbed her by the wrist hard. "Who knows about this? The letters? The visits?"

"No one." Tekla tried to pull away.

"Does Franek know?"

"No."

"Does Franek know!"

"No. No one but me."

He hushed her. "Where are the letters?" Andrzej looked around the room trying to find where she'd hidden them.

"Where were you, Andrzej?" Tekla pressed.

"Why did you not tell me about these letters before?" Andrzej was at her dresser, fishing through her box of stockings.

"Why didn't you tell anyone you were supposed to be in South Carolina? That you weren't in Europe?"

"Stop it."

"That you were pulled out of the battalion before it shipped out."

"Stop it!" He clamped his hands over his ears trying to drown out her voice. "Where are the letters?" he yelled.

Telka held his stare, until his eyes yielded. She marched to the bedside table and removed a bundle of envelopes from the bottom drawer and handed them to him.

"Do not tell anyone of these," he ordered. "Ever. Do

not tell them where I was. Where I was supposed to be. I am a hero to them, Tekla. A hero. Your husband, Andrzej Kowalczyk, a hero."

"You are a coward." She turned and left him with the letters.

12

The biggest challenge Ty faced was finding time to work on those oak pieces hidden in the back corner. Even with his father playing cards every afternoon, Ty couldn't be sure when he'd return home, so he only worked on those pieces late at night after his father went to bed. Then, no matter how tired his body, Ty forced himself through the night. For the first time he chugged mug after mug of steaming coffee to push away the sleep and cold.

Those night sessions passed in a blur. Ty functioned almost instinctually, his body and mind hovering between sleep and consciousness. By morning he was often shocked to find carvings of complex designs that he never would have conceived during the day. But there were plenty of mistakes when sleep overpowered him. Panels snapped. Surfaces scratched. Hands gouged. Many nights, after his frustration and anger subsided, Ty was glad he had purchased extra lumber for his father's table.

One night he left a carved leg out on the bench. When he carried his exhausted body into the barn the next morning, his father was already there, sanding the very piece that was a part of his gift. Ty didn't know if he should ask for it back or just take it from him. As he debated, his father stepped over to him.

"I could not find the others. I guess this is the first." His father handed the leg back to Ty, not realizing the significance of the piece.

Finally after all of those weeks of working, the oak table was assembled. Its beauty was in its simplicity. It was free from the gaudy excesses that adorned merchants' estates. It stood sixteen inches tall and ran four feet by two feet, the perfect size to fit in front of his family's sofa. Its corner legs rose like mighty columns, from solid three-inch square bases. Eight flutes spanned the length of each shaft. Perched atop these legs was the tabletop, comprised of eight trapezoidal half-inch thick panels, each stretching twenty-two inches along its widest base, eighteen inches along its shortest. Four of these were joined together along their diagonals to form a square frame. The two frames placed side by side formed a squared figure-eight and were held together from the underside with stopped-lap dovetail interlocks. This was all corralled by two-inch thick side panels. Each side carved in intricate detail with intertwining grooves.

Beneath the tabletop a single piece of the finest solid oak, three-quarters of an inch thick, served as the bottom shelf. Its corners connected into the square bases of the legs with wooden dowels. Ty succeeded with his creative challenge of assembling the entire table with flat miter joints, dovetail interlocks, and dado joints. Not a single metal nail or screw was used. Every piece had been stained a rich dark brown and sealed with a thin coat of varnish. This exquisite work could grace anyone's home, but Ty would give it to his father, as soon as he added one final touch.

The next morning Andrzej saw his son hunched over the workbench, sound asleep.

"Get up!"

Ty snapped awake and snatched a partially carved leg and metal file in front of him.

"We need to finish three tables today," Kowalczyk pressed with a new urgency, "and you are sleeping like a baby. Never before have I seen a boy waste so much of the day sleeping. I should have stayed with Franek."

Andrzej paced around the barn. He floated back to the staining area and mixed a can that wasn't going to be used. Then he meandered around the sanding table and sorted through finished pieces. He hovered back around Ty and accused him of nodding off again.

All the time, he couldn't get Tekla's words out of his mind.

She had crippled Kowalczyk. He had stopped going to Pulaski Hall. He didn't want to see Franek. He avoided being in the barn where even the money Ty brought in didn't interest him. He wanted to lock himself in his bedroom and see no one, but he couldn't give the impression that something was wrong. Instead, Andrzej retreated to a back corner of the barn and started working on his first table since he returned home. Simple rectangular legs and a standard top. What a disgrace.

A couple days later Andrzej flinched at a knock on the barn door. He whirled around expecting to see military officials. Nikolas Woznicki poked his head through the doorway.

"What do you want?" Kowalczyk snapped.

Woznicki stepped inside and shook Andrzej's hand. He glanced at the table Andrzej was working on.

"This is not for you," he said.

Woznicki laughed. "Your tables are all right, Kowalczyk, but I'll wait for Ty to finish mine."

Andrzej glared at the insult. "What is it, Nikolas?"

"I'm heading to play cards. We can walk together."

"I am very busy."

"Busy? You're standing around."

"It is my break."

"Come on, Kowalczyk," Woznicki joked, "you're the

boss. Leave the work to your master builder."

"Not today," Andrzej repeated, "I have many tables to build."

"There isn't much left, father," Ty offered with a smile. "I'll be fine without you."

"I was not talking to you," Andrzej barked.

Ty's face scrunched, confused and apologetic. He turned back to his carving.

Andrzej saw the furrowed brow on Woznicki's face and played his comment off as a joke. "Boys do not know all of the work involved in business."

Woznicki smiled back politely. "I was also wondering if we could talk for a bit. I got a letter from Jerod today saying how many soldiers were lost in their last battle."

"I do not have time for such things."

Woznicki was lost in his own thoughts. "He is very afraid. I just wanted to hear your thoughts about what it's like."

"Not now."

"Oh." Woznicki's face fell. He lingered, and his eyes glossed over.

"What?" Kowalczyk snapped.

Woznicki shrugged and shook his head. "Nothing." He paused. "Could you at least tell that story of the village greeting you? That is a good story."

Andrzej sighed. He sat down on a stool and rushed through the story about the crowds and the great feast that was prepared.

Then he broke off when he saw Tekla stepped into the barn.

Woznicki's eyes followed Andrzej's. "Good afternoon, Tekla," he called out.

"Hello, Nikolas."

"Andrzej, continue with your story."

Kowalczyk couldn't take his eyes from his wife who

stood on the far side of the barn, watching. "Break time is over," he said. "My family is ready to work, right Tekla?"

"This is your time," she said dryly. "Don't stop your story for me." She stepped over to Ty.

Contempt burned across Andrzej's face. "No. I must work."

Woznicki shifted awkwardly. "All right, Kowalczyk." He stood up from his chair. "Perhaps later in the week we can talk about Jerod's letter."

"Maybe," Andrzej replied, eyes still fixed on his wife.

Nikolas Woznicki let himself out.

"Do not embarrass me in front of the men." Andrzej snarled.

Tekla stepped away from the bench and held his stare. Her voice was calm and challenging. "I said nothing to embarrass you. You feel embarrassed because of you. You know they are lies, but you tell them anyway."

"Do not talk to me that way."

"At least I talk to you. I tell you the truth. You, you tell me nothing. I deserve respect, Andrzej, but you refuse to give it." Tekla turned and marched to the door.

"I am not done talking to you," he yelled after her.

But his wife was gone.

Kowalczyk clasped his forehead, massaging the throbbing pain.

"What's mother talking about?" Ty peeped up.

"It is none of your business. Finish that order."

Ty turned away. He gathered the pieces together and walked to the door.

"Where are you going?" Kowalczyk charged.

"I have a problem with this design, and Mother said she'd help."

Kowalczyk's teeth clenched.

Nikolas Woznicki grumbled to himself the whole walk to Pulaski's, upset that his idle friend couldn't make time to discuss his son's letter. Inside he sat down at the bar and ordered a beer. Woznicki never intended to begin such talk about his friend, but he sat next to Jan Zubek,.

Zubek was a constant emission of negativity and irritation. He took every statement as a personal offense. Compliment and insult alike, if a person said something about him it was an attack against his integrity. And that wasn't limited just to comments about him. Even declarations about other things were blatant comparisons to highlight his own personal deficiencies. The blowing winds at night. The birth of a neighbor's child. The barking of a stray dog. The way his eggs were prepared in the morning. All of these were flagrant insults.

So when Woznicki complained to the bartender about Kowalczyk, Zubek couldn't help but throw in his own uninvited gripes whenever he saw fit.

"He won't talk to me about my boy either. Just because Leone's not off on some secret mission like he was. I could've done what he did if it wasn't for Mrs. Zieczyk's wretched horse. That mule's always out to get me."

Zubek cut off the bartender. "I work harder than Kowalczyk ever has. But do I have a son as talented as Ty who can carry my business? No. I'm stuck with that lout God cursed me with. If my son had a quarter of the brains Kowalczyk's boy does, I'd be running the South End."

He interrupted Woznicki. "He's got too much work to do? My eye. You know why he doesn't come around here any more. Because we're not good enough for him. I heard he's been off meeting with the well-to-do on Center. That's right. That's where he's been all these afternoons."

He interjected to Sal Krymski seated beside him. "Did you hear how he refused to be interviewed by the *Sztandar*? The paper I read isn't big enough for him. He needs a paper that's seen by everyone in town. Waiting for his headline and picture in the *Times*. I wouldn't wipe my shoes with that edition."

He blurted out to no one. "And another thing: two days ago he demanded, that's right, demanded that Sczesniak and Kazek stop telling his stories to anyone else around the neighborhood. Can you believe that arrogance? He thinks he's the only one who can talk about his heroics. I can remember a story just as good as anyone."

For the most part, the men at Pulaski's simply shook their heads and laughed off Zubek's complaints (which, of course, brought on a whole new barrage of his rants). But as they listened to him more and more that afternoon, the men around the bar, while not believing his words entirely, remembered times over the last couple weeks when they saw those same traces of arrogance in Andrzej Kowalczyk.

Kowalczyk decided he would give himself one more week. One more week to push Ty and raise as much money as he could to get out of town. It would only be a matter of time, he thought, before one of the men at Pulaski's spread those foolish stories to someone at the local armory. Once they found out, that information was sure to get back to the regional offices in Detroit. The thought of being captured, though, wasn't what most troubled Kowalczyk. He had to find a way to make sure Franek wouldn't discover his stories, especially now that his brother envied him and his business. If he could find a way to maintain that, the rest didn't matter. He just needed to—

A sharp tug pulled at Andrzej's sleeve and broke his concentration.

"Father," Stanley chastised, looking up from his typed pages, "you're not even listening."

"What?"

"To my story about you and the French battalion."

"Who do you tell these to?" Andrzej lashed at his son.

Stanley's face crumpled. "What?"

"These stories. Who do you tell?"

A smile slid across his son's face. "To Miss Noonan and the kids in my class and Dziadzia Toporski and to the people on my route and—"

"Stop telling these to people."

Stanley's brow furrowed. "Why?"

"Because there is much work to do in the barn, and you are wasting time with that contraption of yours."

"I work a lot in the barn," Stanley insisted.

Andrzej grabbed his son's collar. "You are not to tell these stories to anyone ever again, do you understand?"

Normally it took four days to travel from Austin to Detroit, but the foreman's belligerent urgency had spurred his supervisors on, and the five men left southern Texas with little money among them. Without funds, it was impossible to catch a train northbound from Austin, so they hitchhiked instead. This was typically an easy means of travel, but with five people, few truckers could carry them all at once. A couple times they split up and met at a designated depot in Dallas and Oklahoma City, but in St. Louis their rides dropped them off twenty-six miles apart. It took eight long days without shelter or food before the men regrouped. From then on, they stuck together in the same vehicle. Unfortunately, this limited them to squeezing into the bed of family pickup trucks, which proved torturously slow. Most pickups only traveled a town or two over. This slow puddle jumping northward across Illinois and Indiana was exacerbated by the light Texas clothing the men wore. The freezing winds howled down from Canada, and the men huddled their chattering teeth and shivering bodies together all the way across the Michigan state line.

By the time they reached Detroit, the supervisors were exhausted, hungry, and hypothermic. They no longer talked about avenging their boss' loss, now they had their own hatred for *el bandido*.

Kowalczyk was walking down 28th Street when an armory official called his name behind him. He picked up his pace along the sidewalk to get away. He kept his eyes focused on the alleyway ahead of him to the right and pushed forward, ignoring the voice's calls. He cut down the back street, and the voice demanded him to halt. Andrzej broke into a full sprint and raced past a row of trash cans. Then he stopped. A fence blocked his escape. He turned around and saw Stash hustling toward him.

"Andrzej, is everything all right?"

Kowalczyk laughed nervously. "Of course. Why would things not be all right?"

"I've been calling you for the last three blocks."

"Everything is fine."

"Tekla was telling me—"

"What has she told you?" Andrzej's eyes flared. "None of it is true."

Stash was confused by the outburst. "Calm down. I

wanted to talk to you about Ty."

"Oh." Kowalczyk collected himself and folded his arms across his chest. "About what?"

"You need to give him a break. He's been working over fourteen hours a day."

"He sleeps during the day," Andrzej charged, "that is what he does."

"That's because he works all night long."

"I have never seen him."

"I'm telling you, he does."

"Stash, he is not a child anymore. He is responsible for running a business."

Stash took a calming breath. "Maybe if you actually did some of the work around the barn yourself, he wouldn't have as much."

"I do things."

"Before or after you play cards?"

Andrzej's face hardened. "It is none of your concern how I spend my time or run my business."

"Run your business? If it wasn't for my sister and Ty, your business would still be as ill-respected as before."

The Great War brought a strong unity to the nation. Citizens bonded together for the common good in proud displays of patriotism. Wagner and Bach were banned from the airwaves. Sauerkraut was renamed liberty cabbage. And every true-blooded American child stoned stray dachshund hounds found in the streets. People around the country willfully accepted the many sacrifices asked of them. Rations on most precious and industrial metals. Meat. Eggs. Wheat. Rubber. Nylon. All in the name of the war effort.

None of these restrictions affected Ty, but there was

one item that he needed to finish his father's gift. So Ty took advantage of another American wartime effort: the black market.

Bay City had its own underground network that reached every neighborhood on both sides of the river. This was Ty's first time dabbling in the market, but Uncle Stash had told him of the countless times he had used it to sell items he'd won in the Catacombs: bottles of expensive liquor, gold bars, a solid silver watch. On Tuesday morning, Ty met with his contact into the Bay City underground. Dziadzia Toporski. There was always someone somewhere in town whose mailman knew about unmentionables that could be obtained for a price. It was only a matter of asking around and finding it. In the end, everyone was happy; the buyer got his product, the seller made some extra cash, and the contact took a cut of the sale.

Three days after Ty made his request, Toporski handed him a slip of paper with an address, a time, and a price.

"Don't mess up on your first time," Toporski warned him, "or it'll be your last time."

Ty couldn't contain his smile and assured Dziadzia he would make the meeting.

"Why do you need these?" Toporski asked.

Ty made sure his father wasn't around and motioned Toporski to follow him. When he peeled back the tarp, Dziadzia's eyes widened with awe. The wooden artwork before him was masterfully carved and detailed, missing only the two pieces of glass that would fit perfectly in the frames of the tabletop.

"Criminy," Toporski gasped, "what a creation."

"How much do I owe you?"

Toporski waved the offer away. "Just promise my order will be half as beautiful. That'll be payment enough."

"Your table by the beginning of next week, you have my word."

That night, twenty minutes after sundown, Ty waited outside an alleyway door on Washington and 6th. A hunched, elderly man on the verge of disintegration stepped out of the factory, hugging a flat wooden box. He shuffled over to Ty and set the box on the ground. Ty handed him thirty-two dollars. The man took the money without a word and disappeared down the alleyway.

After his father went to bed that night, Ty stoked the stove in the barn and cleared a spot on the workbench where he spread out a clean towel. The box top pried back easily. Ty removed the two glass panes and held them up to the light. Each two-foot square piece was three-quarters of an inch thick and free of nicks and blemishes.

Ty yawned as he placed the panes on the towel and wiped their surfaces with a kerosene-dampened rag. He marked off the excess edges and laid a metal straight-edge across the glass. The blade of the glass cutter rolled along each side of the transparent pane, leaving a milky groove. Ty slid the piece to the edge of the workbench and, with one quick motion, snapped the unnecessary glass free. He repeated this seven times until both panes were eighteen-by-eighteen inch squares. These glass pieces slid perfectly into the tabletop.

The gift was complete.

Cianek called the raise and tossed four chips into the pot. "What do you have?"

Kowalczyk laid down his hand. "Twos and sixes."

Cianek laughed. "Three jacks." He reached out and pulled the chips in. "Don't look so sad Kowalczyk. It's just one hand."

Hryniewicz picked up the cards and shuffled them. "Yes, Kowalczyk, God blesses you kindly."

"What do you mean?" he asked as he picked up his new hand.

"You'll never have to work again," Hryniewicz said. "With Ty running your business, you can just wait for him to fill your pockets."

"He and I run it together."

Kreska chuckled.

"What?"

"Come on, Andrzej," he said, "your tables are simple. Ty's an expert carpenter."

"He took your business and did things you've never been able to do with it," Josef Sczesniak added.

"It is a family business." Kowalczyk interjected. "I taught him everything he knows."

"You've taught him more than you know," Cianek jabbed.

The men laughed.

"That boy is the boldest man in your family," Woznicki said. "Telling Franek the arrangement is over. That is real leadership."

"And where is Franek?" Hryniewicz asked. "He doesn't come around at all. His pride is too damaged for drinking now."

"Thrown out of the family business by his nephew."

Andrzej glared.

"Oh, don't worry, Kowalczyk. We're only joking," Cianek said. "It doesn't matter if your son runs your business. You're a war hero now."

"Tell us about your time in Paris again," Kreska asked.

"Yes, that's my favorite story."

"I will not tell that story ever again," he snapped, discarding two cards.

The men exchanged looks.

"I will admit, Kowalczyk," Sczesniak said, "before, I had little respect for you, but now I am honored to play cards with a war hero."

13

Kowalczyk muttered a string of curses to himself as he marched up the driveway from Pulaski's that evening. He didn't care that he lost most of his money. He would not tolerate Ty's disrespect of him anymore. Andrzej flung open the barn door.

His son sprang to his feet in the middle of the work area. A long box covered by a tarp was behind him.

"Why are you not working?"

"I have something for you, father. Wait one second." Ty dashed out of the barn, yelling for mother and Stanley.

Kowalczyk stepped over to the covered object and yanked the tarp off. His eyes widened. It was unlike anything Andrzej had ever seen. He walked around it, admiring the flawless flow of grain. The seamless joints. The glass panes placed securely. He squatted down and ran his hand against the surface, streaking his finger across one of the panes. Running footsteps stomped back into the barn, and Kowalczyk stood up. Tekla and Stanley hustled in behind Ty.

"What is it?" Tekla inquired.

"Oh," Ty said disappointedly. "You've already looked."

"I can not believe it," Andrzej's voice whispered.

"I made that gift for you," Ty said.

Andrzej's tone hardened. "I can not believe this. You make me look like a fool."

Ty's brow scrunched. "What?"

"Making me look like an unskilled gypsy. Is that

126

what you think I am?"

"No, father, that isn't what I think at all."

"That is what the men at Pulaski's think. What did you tell them while I was away?"

"Nothing."

"They say my business is no good. My tables are no good. You are better in every way. You outsell me. You build better."

"I've improved the skills you taught me. "

Andrzej stabbed his finger at the table. "That is not how I taught you to build a table."

"I spent three months on this. I bought the best oak and carved it myself. I cut the glass."

"We do not have money to waste on glass."

"Your table was worth it."

Kowalczyk threw his arms to the side. "There, I am wrong again."

"We finally have enough money," his son explained. "You have worked for years, and never once built a table for yourself. Everything was always shipped away, decorating someone else's house. This one is for you. To keep."

"This is not what I want. My tables are simple. None of this fancy design. People do not have money to waste on this."

"You know that's not true. Even today, we got two new orders."

"We did better selling through Franek's store."

"We didn't, father. That was when we struggled. When me and Stan quit school."

Kowalczyk growled. "I put food on the table, clothes on your back, a roof over your head. That sounds fine to me."

"Yes, you did. But Uncle Franek took advantage of you, cheated you out of money that should have been yours."

127

Andrzej's face hardened. "Franek never took advantage of me. He is family and always paid me a fair price."

"He didn't. Why won't you accept that?"

"When I sold tables to Franek, I did not have to hide my face in public. Never once. But now I can not walk through town without someone telling me how my son is better. Franek thought my work was good, but obviously it was not good enough. My son has improved it."

"That's not what I'm saying."

"You offered my tables to Franek as a joke. To stick him with my simple tables, while yours are so good."

Ty's face broke with painful guilt, and his voice came out a whisper. "That wasn't how I meant it, father."

"Your face shows it is true."

Kowalczyk glared at his son. "You have insulted my work and shown everyone how poorly I run my business. You embarrass me, disregard my rules, let your mother work in my barn, send your brother to school. Nothing I say here has meaning. I must be a fool, and my son has corrected me. Here is what I think of this table." Andrzej spat upon it.

Ty's jaw clenched, and his eyes glossed with tears.

"Get this out of my sight," Kowalczyk hissed, "and get back to work, building tables the way I showed you." He turned and stormed out of the barn into the clearing.

Telka ran after him, livid at his actions, but Andrzej ignored her words and stomped up the porch steps.

In the distance, the barn door slammed shut. Then, the electric saw roared to life.

14

Hours later, just before dinner, Tekla walked out to the barn. The saw still buzzed away, biting through a fresh board.

"Ty," she called. "Ty, dinner's ready."

There was no response.

"Ty?"

Tekla glanced in through the window and saw her son feeding a plank through the table saw, its blade eating through the pulpy flesh. She walked back to the kitchen, where Stanley was putting biscuits on the table.

"Go ahead," Telka said as she grabbed a plate from the table and filled it with cabbage and sausage.

"What are you doing?" Andrzej demanded.

She had nothing to say to him. She scooped boiled potatoes onto the plate.

"That is not how I showed him to build," Andrzej complained.

Tekla stepped outside and walked across the clearing to the barn. "Ty." She tried to lift the latch on the door. It was locked from inside. "I brought you a plate."

He didn't respond.

"It's here on the stool."

Tekla waited for a moment, then set the plate down and returned to the house.

Tekla bolted up from bed late that night. "Andrzej,

did you hear that?"

A dismissive grumble answered her concern. He rolled away and pulled the blanket over his shoulder. Tekla slid out of bed, grabbed her robe, and shuffled into the kitchen. She looked out the back door. The clearing was bleached with moonlight. Tekla moved into the living room and peered through the window. No one was in the front yard. She tightened the cord around her waist and headed to the boys' bedroom. She flipped on the light. The room was empty.

"Ty? Stanley?"

She stepped back into the dark hallway, and a burst of light poured from the opened bathroom door. A groggy Stanley turned off the switch and trudged up the hall.

"Stanley, where's Ty?"

He shrugged and slipped past her into his room.

Tekla turned and hurried through the back door into the crisp night air. Her bare feet skipped across the frosty clearing toward the barn where the untouched dinner plate still sat.

"Ty." She pulled at the door handle. It didn't open. Tekla pounded against the barn. "Ty! Are you in there?"

There was no response.

She placed her ear against the door and heard the faint whirl of the electric saw motor. She rushed to the side of the barn and glanced through the window. Blood dripped from the table saw.

"Oh Lord. Andrzej!" Tekla ran to the chopping block and snatched the axe from its perch and raced to the door. She swung it back with all of her strength and launched it. The blade bounced off the wood. She drove the axe over and over and over again, slowly chipping away at the door, until the upper half of it splintered to pieces.

She screamed out to her husband and unlocked the latch and threw the door open.

Ty laid on the ground beside the electric saw, curled up, his back toward Tekla. She ran to her son, dropped to her knees, and lifted him into her arms. His head turned toward her in a daze of slowness. His eyes glossed over, his lips mumbling incoherent sounds. That was when she noticed the pool of blood between her son and the saw.

"Everything will be fine, Ty. Everything will be fine."

Ty reached up, and Tekla coiled back. Blood gushed everywhere. His right arm was hacked to the bone at the wrist. She tried to hold back her tears and clutched Ty tightly, yelling out for Andrzej, for anyone to come and help.

Kowalczyk finally shuffled into the threshold of the barn, embittered. "Why are you yelling?"

Then his eyes widened, and his entire body went weak.

"Go get help!" Telka urged him.

"What happened to my son?" Andrzej stepped closer, his hands cupped over his mouth.

"Go get Dr. Brown! Now!"

He leaned against the wall and vomited. "Oh my son. My son." Andrzej doubled over, sobbing.

Tekla rose to her feet and dragged her husband to Ty and ran from the barn through the clearing and almost tripped over Stanley who had shuffled into the night.

"Mother, what's wrong?" he asked, rubbing his eyes.

She knelt down. "Stanley, run to Dr. Brown's as fast as you can. Do you understand?"

"You're bleeding," Stanley cried, reaching for her robe.

"There's been an accident. Ty's hurt. We need a doctor."

Stanley nodded his head and dashed away barefooted.

"And get Uncle Stash," she yelled after he disappeared into the darkness. Tekla looked down at her robe stained with Ty's blood. She closed her eyes and took a deep breath, then hurried back to the barn. Andrzej sat inside, weeping, rocking Ty in his arms. He looked up and saw Tekla.

"Do not let Stanley come in here. This is not right for a boy to see," he muttered through tears, "not right for a boy to see his father like this."

Tekla stepped beside them, knelt down, and pulled Ty away from Andrzej. She stroked her son's cheek.

Part Three

1

Two nights later, winter crept across the Saginaw River Valley, and clouds leaked clumps so large and moist they slopped the streets and drenched every tree in Bay City. For hours, the temperature wavered between slush and snow, but the winds from Canada eventually petrified the land. Roads crystallized into frozen trails of muck. Icy shells encased unsheltered cars. The snowstorm continued for the rest of the night, accumulating in two foot drifts that rose with the sun over the South End.

That morning, families from the Polish neighborhood put on their best coats and hats and attended Ty Kowalczyk's funeral. By the time Doctor Brown had arrived, Ty had lost so much blood there was little that could be done to save him. Father Hedwig of St. Stanislaus Church led the services at the cemetery and spoke about souls being taken for grander reasons. This offered little comfort to the mourners. They endured the loss and the cold as they wondered about life taken away so senselessly.

All of this passed by Andrzej Kowalczyk in a blur. He couldn't piece together the day. Surely, he wasn't to blame for what had happened, he thought. Ty must have fallen asleep while working. He had asked Tekla, but she hadn't spoken to him since that night in the barn. She wasn't swept up in the daze of sorrow and suffering that he'd anticipated. Instead, an anger simmered in her eyes. He was certain she was going to tell the men at

Pulaski's about his stories, or notify the armory he was home, or tell Franek he was a fraud. How can she hold that against me, he wondered, as his son was lowered into the ground.

Kowalczyk walked home from the cemetery alone and retreated into his bedroom. He had already spent days lying in his bed staring at the ceiling. Tekla had moved her things to the boys' room. Nobody had looked in on him.

Another two days passed before Andrzej left his bed. His throat had grown parched from the dry winter air, and he went into the kitchen. Tekla and Stash sat at the dining room table, talking. Andrzej stepped toward the ice box, and an explosion of pain smashed into his nose. He dropped to the floor, and Stash drove his boot into Kowalczyk's ribs and stomach and head. Tekla screamed for her brother to stop, but the blows continued until she forced her way between the two men and shoved Stash back. Her brother slammed his fist against the tabletop, snatched his coat from the rack, and stormed out the back door.

Andrzej wiped the blood from his nose and eased himself against the wall, massaging the pain in his chest. "Thank you."

His wife glared at him. "I won't let you take Stash from me too by dying at his hands." She left him sprawled on the floor.

Kowalczyk pulled himself to his feet, limped into the bedroom, and grabbed the small canister from his dresser. He knew how much was there even before counting it, but he did so anyway, senselessly hoping to find enough to get out of town. He had been so close before, but those damn card games and the bills for the funeral—

Andrzej closed his eyes. He would find the money somehow.

The power of a grudge is unequaled in its pervasive decay. It festers and rots a person away from the inside until only a hollow shell remains. The embittered memories of past wrongs become inseparable from a person's temperament, and any attempt to correct the situation is an unforgivable act of weakness. At least, that was how Franek Kowalczyk viewed it.

But he did believe there were rare times when a grudge became unnecessary, even absurd. Those moments made a person realize that lifetimes were too short to exert one's energy and endurance on that type of hatred. When he learned of Ty's passing, Franek said a prayer for his nephew. He attended the funeral and couldn't stop his tears as the casket sunk into the earth. Despite his bold pride, Ty had been the most talented carpenter Franek had ever met. And for that, he respected him.

That respect, though, Franek would never give to his brother.

"Advance?" He slammed down his pen. "Get out of my store."

"Please, Franek."

"You have your profits and reputation. Use those."

"Ty's funeral was so much. I need money for that loan."

"I don't give a damn about your loan."

"I will sell you tables again," his brother pleaded, "cheaper than what you paid me before."

Franek dismissed this with a wave.

"Please, I will do anything you ask. I will build faster. Stanley will quit school tomorrow."

"He's a boy. What can he do?"

"Tend to the small things, like he did before."

Franek shook his head.

"Tekla will help too."

He looked Andrzej in the eye. "Your tables are worthless, shoddy pieces. I will never sell them again."

"I have some of Ty's tables. You can buy some of those."

"Get out of my store!"

Andrzej hesitated, about to say something, but turned for the door.

Kowalczyk pulled on his overalls and thick jacket and braved the painful cold of the barn. He swung back the splintered door, stepped inside, and flipped on the overhead switch. In the flash of light, he caught a glimpse of the splattered table saw, looming like a torture device with its fanged blade jutting out from its metal base. Andrzej looked away, trying to keep his back to the machine, and walked to the frozen Franklin stove. He piled kindling and discarded legs inside the furnace and lit a match. The scrap wood caught, and Andrzej blew gently on the struggling flames until they crackled with life. The stove breathed out heat that pushed away the aching chill.

Kowalczyk rubbed his hands together and turned around. The deadly saw leapt out, and he flinched back. He grabbed a shovel from the side wall and dug into the dirt that was crusted with his son's blood. He hauled it outside and tossed it into a tall snowdrift. It took a dozen trips to remove the blood and frozen vomit from the ground. Then Andrzej moved to the frozen pools of blood scarring the top and sides of the table saw. The ones closest to the stove were starting to thaw with a glossy, moist skin. They could have been spilled varnish, Kowalczyk thought, the rich brownish-red color and gummy consistency—

Andrzej cleared his head and picked up a putty knife from the workbench. The leech-sized wounds peeled up surprisingly clean as Kowalczyk scraped the top and sides, wiping the gobs into a rag. He finished the flat surfaces quickly, but the blade itself, with its jagged teeth and claws and fangs and talons, that would be impossible. As he inspected the blade closer, Andrzej saw, frozen to one of the teeth, a morsel of his son's flesh.

Vomit splattered on the ground. Kowalczyk wiped his hand across his mouth and lowered himself to one knee until he could control the trembling.

Andrzej staggered outside and scooped snow into his mouth and rinsed the rancid taste away. Then he packed a large ball of snow together and carried it back into the barn. He spread a clean rag across the top of the furnace and set the snow on it. The ball hissed with steam and slowly deflated, melting into the cloth. Kowalczyk snatched the dripping rag from the furnace, twirled it into a long roll, and flossed back and forth, back and forth between every tooth of the saw. When he finished, he threw the rag into the fire and shoveled the fresh vomit outside.

Back in the carving area of the barn, Andrzej found enough of Ty's panels and shelves and legs and moldings to complete ten tables. Few of the pieces were sanded or stained, but he and Stanley could easily finish those. Kowalczyk rummaged through the remaining piles and collected an assortment of legs. They were all partially carved, and he cursed Ty's unpredictable method. Some of them had tops that were finished with flutes and curves, but the bottoms were untouched; other legs had been etched from top to bottom but only half way around. Piled off to the side were partially carved boards stretching four, six, eight feet in length. A smile eased across his face. He could cut those into squares and circles and ovals and triangles and preserve most of the original carving, then match them together with the legs and create completed tables. He could use the finished side panels to hide the uncarved parts of the legs. It was a perfect plan. Andrzej clumped pieces together and discovered he had enough for five more tables. He calculated how much he would make filling fifteen of Ty's orders. It would be more than enough to start his life over again somewhere else.

Excited with these prospects, Kowalczyk grabbed one of the partially carved tabletops, hauled it to the saw, and flipped on the power switch. The blade spun to life, and a spray pelted his face. Andrzej lurched back and wiped the back of his hand across his cheek. Blood stained his skin. He rushed to the broken piece of mirror hanging from the back wall and examined his face and neck. There was the bruise from Stash's boot and splattered blood, but no lacerations. He brushed his face against his sleeve and returned to the machine and shut it off. His eyes fixed on the spinning blade that flashed red, silver, red, silver, red, silver, red until it slowed to a stop. Andrzej rotated the motionless blade and stared at half of it, the half that had been hidden in the base of the saw when he had cleaned it. It was still stained with Ty's thawed blood. Kowalczyk's lips curled as pain and rage quivered inside him. He snatched a cloth tarp beside him and flung it over that hideous saw. He stepped away from the machine and backed into something.

Behind him was the table Ty had built.

2

The war is pure and clean from two-thousand feet up, and pilots are the heroes everyone wants to be. The new recruits from the States show up with their fur-lined leather coats, polished boots, and pressed uniforms, their scarves blowing back in the wind. They've read the manuals and they think they're ready to fly. They talk about gallant knights and flying steeds and jousting tournaments overhead. That's their vision of dogfights. Who fills their heads with such shit?

You talk to anyone here who's flown and they'll tell you no one lives past his first six weeks. And that's mostly true. Two-thousand feet high, you've got nothing but wood, canvas, and wire keeping you from falling to the ground. You take a round of enemy fire and there's nothing left to grab that isn't dropping fast. And once those bullets start at you, you're crazy mad with fear and murder and you don't have time to notice the brandy and milk puked on your instrument panel or the piss and shit you're sitting in. You're too busy trying to get a kill. Not for the glory, just to keep yourself alive. To keep yourself from helping that Hun become an ace. First one to five wins.

I've killed a man, Amelia. Out on my third run. I meant to tell you about it, but he just dropped out of the clouds, guns firing. I banked and circled behind him and caught him in my sights. My tracers tore through his wing and engine, and the plane burst into flames. The dead weight pulled him down, and I caught a glimpse of his wide eyes, that pale look of dread when the pit of his stomach started sinking, telling him it was over. The plane sucked him down and his mouth opened wider than I thought possible, screaming a never-ending string of curses and prayers to his god. That was when I looked away, unable to bear the sight any longer. The sight of what my hands had done.

I was never happier to have my feet on the ground than that afternoon. But once you land, death is all around you. You get that first whiff, and the stench lingers in your memory forever. The mess halls are the worst. Dozens and dozens of men with that smell clinging to them, in their clothes and skin. They can't escape it. All day long, burrowing through trenches with filth and guts. They're nothing more than rats with blood-shot eyes, scurrying around just to gain two-hundred yards of land. The trenches are big open tombs where the dead and yet-to-be-dead share space, filled with generations of dead, sons and fathers and grandfathers, all adding to the stench.

Those who aren't lucky enough to die are hauled around on stretchers to the ambulances that have doors smeared with the stains of piss and butchershop blood. I wish I could get that image out of my mind.

I used to tell pilots I was from Bay City and what we built. I've never made more enemies faster in my life. No joke. Every pilot has lost a buddy in a DH-4. Out here they call them the Flying Coffins, because that's how they come down, engines erupting in flames for no reason. I defended Bay City, saying we only made the wings and had nothing to do with the engines, but nobody cares about that distinction. A Flying Coffin is a Flying Coffin. I don't tell pilots where I'm from anymore.

These are the heroes nobody wants to know. But I guess as long as everyone ignores the uncontrollable tick in our cheeks or the twitching in our hands, they can believe whatever the hell they want.

Please forgive me, Rupe

She traced her eyes over his writing and held the letter like it was the small of his back. She was always relieved to reread his letters, no matter how gory or gruesome. The contents were less graphic than the things she imagined in the war. It wasn't that Amelia Noonan was an excessive worrier; she handled the information from the front with remarkable poise. Her imagination was just so active and vivid that she envisioned the events in Europe in epic proportions with tragic and heroic details.

She found few people who were willing to discuss the stories whispered about the War. They dismissed the topic because she was a lady. But she knew that their own fears were the reasons for their hesitancy. That was why Amelia shared selected parts of Rupert's letters with her students. Their attentive ears and eager questions gave her the needed interaction she couldn't find with adults.

A light rapping rattled the back door of the schoolhouse, and Amelia called the visitor in. A man hesitantly poked his head inside.

"Good afternoon, Mr. Kowalczyk," Amelia said with a smile. "Come in."

Her visitor inched into the classroom and removed his hat.

"What happened to your eye?" she asked.

"I slipped on some ice."

"Are you all right?"

"Yes, yes." He walked toward her desk.

"We missed Stanley today," she said, offering him a seat.

Mr. Kowalczyk waved her offer away. "I do not want to bother you long."

"It's no trouble," she said as he glanced around. "I'm sorry to hear about Ty's accident. He was such an amazing artisan. Stanley's always talked about how his brother made your business so successful."

Mr. Kowalczyk's jaw clenched.

"Your family is in my prayers."

Her visitor cleared his throat. "We need Stanley to be at home to work for the business."

She had expected these words when he first walked in. "That must have been a difficult decision for you and Mrs. Kowalczyk to make."

His eyes drifted downward, his lips twisting. "I should be going."

"Your son has a remarkable talent writing stories."

"He will not have time for stories anymore," Mr. Kowalczyk said as he secured his hat.

"That's unfortunate." Amelia couldn't keep the disappointment from her voice. "Please tell Stanley he can visit whenever he gets a chance."

He muttered that he would and turned for the door.

"Mr. Kowalczyk," she stood up from her desk, "and if you have any time, I'm sure the children would love to hear about your experiences in Europe."

He swallowed hard, and his eyes seemed to quiver. "I am sorry. I can not do that."

Andrzej tapped the final nail into the wood and stepped back from his first finished table. It was expertly designed and finely crafted. Andrzej didn't care that he hadn't carved any of the pieces; sanding, staining, and hammering were contribution enough.

The splintered barn door flew open, and Tekla stormed in. "How dare you take Stanley out of school and end his paper route without discussing it with me."

Andrzej retreated behind the Franklin stove.

"He's going back tomorrow."

"I have to fill Ty's orders."

"He doesn't need to be taken out of school to sand and stain."

"I can not do it all myself."

"I don't care for you reasons. You better hope I can get his route back." She turned to leave.

"I need him here," Kowalczyk called after her. "And you too."

She spun back around. "I will have nothing to do with that money you need."

"But I—" Andrzej stopped. He didn't want to push Tekla. That would only anger her into revealing his secrets, so he yielded to her words. Kowalczyk would find a way to force Stanley to get the tables done. He would find a way.

———

A knock banged at the kitchen door. Dziadzia Toporski waved from the other side of the glass and let himself in. "I come bearing gifts," he announced, shaking the snow from his overcoat. Ned Linkowski, who ran the stables on 24th Street, stepped in behind him.

"I brought that spare door Tekla asked me about," Linkowski said. "Do you want to take care of that now?"

"Fine."

Toporski handed a bundle of mail to Andrzej. "Criminy, Kowalczyk, what happened to your eye?"

He rifled through the letters, checking for anything from the armory. "I walked into a cupboard door."

"I did that once years ago. That's always a stinger," Toporski chuckled. "I wanted to ask if it'd be okay to bring Ignasiu over this week?"

"Who?"

"Henrik Sinicki's oldest."

Kowalczyk shrugged. "Why?"

"I told you that night at Pulaski's. He was in the

Regiment and came home injured and hasn't left his bedroom since. Henrik and Ana think if he talks to someone who's been through a similar experience, he might come around."

Andrzej shook his head. "Not this week."

Toporski smiled encouragingly. "When Ignasiu heard it was the hero from the South End, he insisted on meeting you. I think it'll be good for the boy."

"It has been a difficult week."

"I know," Toporski said respectfully. "You tell me when you're ready. I think it'll be good for both of you."

Thick flakes fell from the sky as Kowalczyk and Linkowski hoisted the replacement door from the cart and hauled it to the barn.

"Normally, I would build this myself," Andrzej explained, "but I haven't—"

"No need to say anything, Kowalczyk. I understand."

They leaned the door against the wall, and Andrzej ducked inside the workshop to grab a couple of screwdrivers and hammers. The men worked in silence, removing the damaged door and attaching the new one. They carried the hacked remains inside the barn and tossed them onto the scrap bin. Linkowski stepped over to the roaring stove and warmed his hands as Kowalczyk fed wood into the fire.

"Is that one of Ty's?" Linkowski asked, pointing to the finished table off to the side.

Andrzej nodded.

"I wish I would've had enough money when Ty took orders before."

"Do you want that one?"

"Really?"

"If you can find the money, it is yours."

"Are you serious, Kowalczyk?"

"I need to sell them quickly."

"I can get you the money in two days. Is that all right?"

"That will be fine."

———

A little after one on Tuesday afternoon, two crisply dressed men glided into Franek's.

"Is this the Kowalczyk store?" the taller man inquired.

"Yes, it is." Franek darted up from his desk and hurried to their side.

"I work for the Clay family, the supervisor at the shipyards," announced the tall man.

"And I'm here on behalf of Mr. Willis, manager of Aladdin Homes on Washington," declared the more portly of the visitors.

A smile widened across Franek's face. "It's a pleasure to meet you both. How can I help you today?"

"Mr. Clay wishes to express his deepest regards at the loss of your son," the tall man sympathized.

"As would Mr. Willis."

"It's not my son."

The two gentlemen exchanged looks. "You said this is the Kowalczyk store, correct?"

"Yes, it is. But Ty, the boy, was my nephew, not my son."

"Oh, terribly sorry, Mr. Kowalczyk, that is my *associate's* mistake," the tall man said, giving a reprehensible look to his companion. "Mr. Clay still sends his sympathies."

The portly gent's face wrung with apology. "As does Mr. Willis."

"Thank you," Franek said with his most sincere nod.

"Both of our employers," the first man continued, "have heard that your nephew made exceptional tables. With his unfortunate passing, they are interested in obtaining some of his final works. We would like to see your selection of his tables."

Franek's smile broke for a slight moment. "I don't have any."

"Oh, that is a shame. Where else can we find some?"

"No, no, I do sell them," Franek stressed. "You see, I just don't currently have any here. I sold my last one yesterday, but I'm expecting more soon."

"When?"

"By the end of the week at the very latest."

"That should be good enough," the tall man deemed.

"I hope your employers understand that there is a limited quantity of pieces left and they tend to be—"

"Price is not an issue for Mr. Clay," the taller man retorted.

"Nor for Mr. Willis."

"I can hold a table for each of you with a down payment."

"As expected." Both men snatched velvet pouches from their pockets and withdrew crisp bills and handed them to Franek. "I assume this will ensure us the best available."

Franek concealed his excitement. "Of course."

The tall man presented a card. "Please contact me as soon as the table arrives."

His cohort offered his own card. "And me."

"I will," Franek assured them. "And if there is anything else your employers need, please tell them Franek Kowalczyk is always at their service."

———————

Franek waded through the deep snow to his brother's

where he found Andrzej and Stanley in the back of the barn, sanding.

His brother stood up from his stool. "Franek?"

"Yes. Don't look so surprised." He navigated through the machinery. "What happened to your eye?"

"Nothing."

Franek stopped beside the finished table. "Is this one of Ty's?"

"Yes."

"How many do you have?"

"Fifteen."

"I'll take all of them."

Andrzej set down the rough panel in his hand. "I do not understand."

"I said I'll buy all of Ty's tables from you. When can you have them ready?"

Kowalczyk pointed to the pieces scattered across the table. "All of them?"

"Yes, Andrzej. I don't have time for games."

"It will take a while."

"I'll need them soon, but I'll take this one tonight and—"

"That one is already sold."

"To whom?"

"Ned Linkowski."

"The stableboy? He doesn't deserve this fine table. I'll give you the four extra dollars I promised you."

"He is paying full price."

Franek huffed in frustration. "Fine. I will match that."

"I already promised it to him."

Franek tapped his fingers on the workbench. "Have you sold the others?"

"No."

"Promise me those, and I will pay you full price for each one."

"That is no better than what everyone else is paying."

Oh, how he still demands more, Franek thought. "Fine. I will pay you full price *and* whatever extra money you need to cover your loan. If you deliver all fifteen tables to me."

His brother paused, contemplating the offer. "But I promised that one to Linkowski."

"Do you want the advance or not?" Franek pushed.

Andrzej rubbed his forehead. "When do you need them?"

"The first two by the end of the day tomorrow and the rest—"

"Tomorrow? That is impossible. We have to sand and stain these and put them together. It will take some time."

"Show me you're the woodworker you promised to be, Andrzej."

His brother grimaced at the thought. "All right. We will have them ready for you by tomorrow evening."

———————

"Tekla!" Andrzej screamed from the living room that night.

His wife ran up behind him. "What? What is it?"

Andrzej pointed. "What is that doing here?"

"That's where it belongs."

"I will not have that thing in my house."

"I'm not moving it."

"But—"

"Andrzej," her voice was uncompromising, "Ty's table will remain in this room."

He exerted a sound that was part scream, part whine. "I will not allow it in here. It is a curse!" he sniveled. "Destroy it. Get rid of it. Anywhere, but not in here."

"You don't mean that."

"Do not tell me what I mean," he snapped.

"It's the last thing Ty made," she said firmly. "We're keeping it."

"Tekla," Andrzej collected himself. He calmed his voice and articulated each word to help her understand, "all I am asking, all I have ever asked, is for people to do as I say. Why does no one understand that? I do not want to see this table," he stressed. "Do you understand me? I do not want—"

"If you think you're the only one who suffers, you are a blind fool. I knew Ty in a way you never did because you were too busy trying to be someone you thought you had to."

He stepped back, pointing at her words. "That is your intention, I knew it. To reveal my stories," he hissed. "That is what you are planning to do."

"I am not."

"You are. Admit it."

"Your lies are an embarrassment to me. I wouldn't tell anyone because that would make it too easy for you to have someone else to blame."

"That is not true."

"You are too weak to admit your lies to anyone."

"I am not afraid," he stammered.

His wife sighed with exasperation and turned to leave the room.

"You do not believe me," Kowalczyk challenged. He grabbed her by the shoulders. "You will see. One day I will tell people the truth. About how I never went to Europe, never fought in the war, never served a single day as a soldier—"

A gasp filled the room. Andrzej turned and saw Stanley in the threshold, hugging the doorjamb. He had heard every word. Stanley bolted backwards, his eyes widened from incomprehensible revelation.

"Stanley, wait!" Andrzej stepped toward him. Stanley looked up, his face aghast from the sight of his father. He backed away and sprinted to his room. Andrzej stared down the empty hallway, and Stanley's door slammed shut.

3

The mud and ice caked his boots as Andrzej trudged through the slop that had once been a road. He fought to pull the loaded cart forward and succeeded in jerks and surges whenever the muck released its grip. He stopped to warm his hands and catch his breath. The delivery was exhausting him. He had worked alone all through the night to finish the other table. No matter how much Andrzej had begged him, Stanley would have nothing to do with the sanding or staining or him. Kowalczyk needed to find a way to keep his son quiet before he spread the news to the people on his paper route. If any of them learned the truth, the armory would surely be the next to know.

"Kowalczyk," someone yelled from the sidewalk, "you should slow down from such great speeds."

Josef Sczesniak, Sal Krymski, and Isaak Grekowicz laughed and squashed through the mud toward him.

"What happened to your eye?" Sczesniak baited him. "Did you lose the fight?"

"I walked into an overhanging board," Kowalczyk said without a smile as the other men chuckled.

"Let us help you," Grekowicz offered.

The three men positioned themselves behind the cart and pushed, freeing the wheels from the mire as Kowalczyk directed the slow but steady roll.

"Are these Ty's tables?" Krymski asked.

"Yes."

"How many do you have left?" Grekowicz called.

"Fifteen total."

"When will mine be finished?" Sczesniak asked.

"There are no more available."

The cart stopped.

Sczesniak stepped to the front. "What do you mean?"

"Franek is buying all of them."

Krymski and Grekowicz trekked forward. "Why?"

"We had great fortune, the Clays and Willises each purchased one."

"The supervisor at the shipyard?"

"Yes."

"The one who fired Zwaska for the German."

Andrzej's face fell. "That is the one."

"Ty should have refused his order," Sczesniak grumbled.

"He did not order from Ty," Kowalczyk blurted.

The men exchanged glances and stared at Andrzej questioningly. "What do you mean?"

"We got the order two days ago," he reluctantly admitted.

"What about the order Ty promised me?" Krymski asked.

Andrzej looked away.

"Well?"

"Franek has already committed new orders to other families on Center."

"So my money means nothing compared to the rich families? Is that what you're saying, Kowalczyk?" Sczesniak challenged.

"No, that is not true."

"Then where are our tables?" Krymski demanded. "I already gave the payment for my purchase."

"So did I."

"I was promised a table."

Andrzej shrugged. "There are no more left. I am sorry."

"I want my deposit back."

Andrzej's brow furrowed.

"Have you already spent our money too?" Krymski asked in disbelief.

"Kowalczyk returns a war hero," Sczesniak proclaimed, "and now he only deals with the wealthy. Zubek was right. His own people are no longer important."

"That is not true," Andrzej protested.

"I want my deposit back."

"Everyone will hear about this, Kowalczyk."

And the three men stormed off, leaving Andrzej alone to drag his cart.

Kowalczyk labored through the streets and arrived at his brother's store just before the sunlight faded from the sky.

"Franek, I wanted to ask—"

"Good news, Andrzej," his brother said as he wiped the last streak of melted flakes from the table's surface, "the Sullivans and the Hudsons ordered tables. I need those by Monday."

Andrzej's shoulders fell. "Yes, that is good." He paused, staring at the floor. "Ty took many orders from people in the community. I need to sell some of the tables to them."

Franek laughed at the thought. "Andrzej, we will make far more money waiting for word to spread up and down Center Avenue. Come here." Franek walked over to his desk, grabbed a stuffed envelope, and counted Andrzej's share.

Kowalczyk looked at the money in his hand. "But the people have already paid deposits. They will not tolerate this."

"Give them back their pennies."

Kowalczyk grimaced.

"You want that advance, don't you?"

By the time Kowalczyk lugged the empty cart home, there were eight people gathered in his kitchen, simmering. Tekla rushed to the door when she saw him, and the demands and complaints erupted behind her. They were not going to leave until they received their orders or their deposits.

"They should understand how few tables are left," Andrzej complained.

"They do understand," his wife replied. "They're angry because you sold a table to the Clays. That they can not accept."

"It is out of my hands."

"That isn't true and you know it. The tables should go to the people who ordered them first."

"That is impossible. The people on Center want Ty's tables. And Franek will give me an advance."

"What do you need the money for?"

Kowalczyk rubbed his temples. "I can not pay them back."

"We owe them that money."

"I will not have enough."

"You will pay them back. You will not drag us down with you. This is my reputation at stake. And Stash's."

Andrzej froze, wincing at the thought of Stash. He took a deep breath. "Can you ask your brother for the list of orders?"

The next day Kowalczyk stared at the names. Yuri Cianek. Cliff Zwaska. Igor Tvardek. Manny Kreska. Sal Krymski. Benya Owsiak. Josef Sczesniak. Dziadzia Toporski. Avery Hryniewicz. Hank Sawicki. So many men who knew his stories. And that didn't include the other twenty-three families from the South End. He was sickened with the thought of telling each Polish customer that his order was going to be shipped to Center Avenue. But he had to do it. He had calculated the numbers three times: all of the money he had plus what Franek was going to give him for the tables was just enough to pay back the deposits he owed to the South End families. Andrzej needed the advance from his brother to have enough money to get out of town.

Andrzej grabbed the stack of money from the table and walked through the living room. Stanley sat on the floor with his head nestled on top of Ty's table, his arms stretched across it, embracing it. Andrzej called out to his son, but Stanley didn't move.

Kowalczyk stepped beside him and squatted down. "There are tables to finish."

Stanley turned his head away and buried it into his arm.

Andrzej felt awkward and cleared his throat. "We can work and talk about stories you *can* tell people."

Stanley snapped his head up. "Stories are lies, and I'm never writing one again."

Kowalczyk flinched at his son's outburst, then collected himself. "I know you are confused right now, but you have to promise me you will not tell anyone what you heard."

Stanley didn't respond.

"Stanislaw," Andrzej demanded, "promise me you will not tell those things ever. Not to the people on your paper route, not to your teacher, not to Dziadzia, not to anyone, do you understand me?"

Stanley's angry eyes glossed over.

"Because if you do, I will have your typewriter destroyed."

4

The door slammed shut, and Kowalczyk leapt awake from the sanding table with a coldness that pained his body.

"Christ, Andrzej, it's freezing in here. Get that fire going."

Andrzej wiped sawdust from his cheek and trudged over to the stove.

"I have three more orders," Franek sang. "My shop is finally making money again." He looked at his brother stoking the embers. "Aren't you happy?"

"Yes, Franek," he replied without emotion, "very happy."

"When can you have those ready for me?"

"I can not do it anymore."

"Don't grow lazy, Andrzej."

"I have not slept for three days, Franek. I am the only one working here. It is too much."

"Ty finished orders without any trouble."

Kowalczyk jammed another log into the stove.

"Here, I'll help." Franek moved to Andrzej's stool at the sanding table and picked up an unfinished panel. "Where are the pieces?"

"That is one in your hand."

"This?" Franek's mouth wrinkled in disgust. "This isn't finished. It's only partially carved."

"I am building some with Ty's pieces and uncarved parts."

"What are you thinking? These customers don't want

any of your pieces."

"That is all I could find."

"You're cheating me out of orders, Andrzej."

"There are still ten complete ones."

"The advance was for fifteen tables."

"Please Franek, I need that money."

His brother folded his arms across his chest, thinking. "Fine. To make up for my loss, we will go back to the original extra four dollars for your payment."

"But—"

"That's the only way you'll get an advance."

"I will not have enough for them. People ask me every day for their deposits back."

"Use part of the advance."

Andrzej sighed, calculating this in his head.

"It's your choice," Franek said.

Kowalczyk wrung his hands. "All right."

"Not another problem, Andrzej. Those last six orders better be perfect. Finished when I ask, completed only with Ty's pieces, is that understood?"

Kowalczyk nodded.

Franek tossed the crude piece onto the workbench, brushed the sawdust from his hands, and headed for the door

"What should I do with the other tables?" Andrzej called after to him.

Andrzej Kowalczyk took the last bite of golabki and carried his plate to the sink to wash it. His dinners had become solitary events, just like his breakfasts and lunches, his sleeping and waking, his work and rest. He stacked the rinsed dishes in the cupboard and noticed the light in the barn. He pulled on his jacket and shuffled through the backyard. Inside he found Tekla perched in the carving area.

"I thought it was empty," he said as he walked toward her. "What are you doing?"

"Carving."

Andrzej watched the knife in her hand move skillfully over the wood, her eyes locked on the rough shape that was evolving into the leg of a table.

"I did not know you were so skilled," he said.

"Who do you think taught Ty how to carve?"

There was a natural ease in the way she attacked the lumber. Every cut precise and confident. "I thought Stash had," he mumbled, watching her work.

"I quit my position at Wilson's today," she stated. "I'm going to work here."

Kowalczyk's throat tightened, and his eyes moistened. He had never felt such appreciation or respect for his wife before. He leaned toward her and, with the utmost humility and relief, whispered, "Thank you."

Tekla set the wood down and looked him in the eye. "I'm not doing this for you, Andrzej. I'm doing this because it's what I've always wanted to do, and I'm not going to let you stop me anymore."

Andrzej stepped back.

"One day," she continued, "someone will discover your lies and take you away. And I won't allow you to destroy this business in the meantime. From now on, I will control how it's run."

Tekla turned back to her carving. There hadn't been a hint of anger or vengeance in her voice, only the unshakable calm of certainty.

And that terrified Andrzej Kowalczyk.

5

He bundled himself up the next morning, stuffed his pockets with money and the list of names, and headed out into the snowstorm. When Milos Brotzclov looked through the window of his front door and saw Kowalczyk, he dismissed him with an offensive gesture and left him in the cold. Andrzej kept knocking until Mrs. Brotzclov answered. Nora was only initially rude but warmed up slightly when she learned she could have one of the five tables that Franek refused. She agreed to the offer, but made it clear that she'd have nothing to do with him if it wasn't for Ty's skill.

The Kazeks, who lived off 32nd Street, were one of the most hospitable families in the neighborhood. They expressed their condolences to Andrzej and offered him a hot meal and cup of coffee. Kowalczyk politely declined, removed his hat, and told them they could purchase a table if they were interested. The Kazeks bubbled with excitement and started to fill a plate for Andrzej to celebrate. He refused the offer and said he had many families to see. The Kazeks insisted he at least take a couple warm paczkis for his journey. Andrzej smiled, accepted the food, and moved on to the next family.

Kowalczyk encountered friendly receptions at the Dzubas and Czaplas, who both were delighted to buy one of Ty's tables. Karl Grznya was next on the list. There was a flash of happiness in his eyes when Andrzej explained he could receive one of Ty's tables.

"When will it be ready?" he asked.

"In a couple months."

His face stiffened. "When? After you finish the others for Center Avenue?"

Andrzej didn't know what to say. Grznya cursed Kowalczyk and accused him of offering a table only as an afterthought. He swore he would never forgive him for how he treated his fellow Poles and demanded his deposit back. Andrzej counted out the bills and offered an apology, but his words sounded forced and insincere. Karl Grznya snorted and told Kowalczyk to enjoy his life with his new rich friends and slammed the door in his face.

The Cianeks were glad to hear they could get Ty's last table and invited Andrzej in. He brushed the snow from his hat and coat and warmed himself with a mug of steaming coffee.

"I know there's much talk about you Kowalczyk," Cianek said, "but you should come to Pulaski's for cards again. Anger is short lived among friends. They'll soon forget, unless you stay away, like your brother."

Andrzej smiled and thanked Cianek for the advice. "Perhaps another night. I still have many people to see."

Kowalczyk set out into the lashing wind and sleet and endured the harsh conditions of apologies, insults, and curses.

There were only a couple stops left when Andrzej arrived at Dziadzia's. Busia let him in, and he apologized for interrupting their dinner. He pulled the money from his pocket and handed it to Toporski, who didn't look up from his plate. "I don't want it."

"What?"

"I don't want that money," he said without bitterness or challenge.

"I do not understand."

Toporski set his fork down and looked Andrzej in

the eye. "Ty was like a grandson to me. I've watched that boy grow up since he was as small as a sugar beet. He promised me a table, and now you're disgracing his word with your greed. I don't want a handful of dollars as my last memory of him. I want something to cherish."

"I do not have any left."

"I've saved from every check, Andrzej, just so I could buy one of your son's tables. If you can't find one for me among those you're selling to the people on Center, keep my money. Obviously, that's most important to you." Dziadzia turned back to his meal and shoveled in a forkful.

The next morning, Kowalczyk returned to the same five families who were going to receive one of Ty's tables. He asked them to take back their deposits so he could sell their order to someone else. The families either refused outright or accused him of trying to sell their pieces to people on Center Avenue. Kowalczyk insisted it was for Toporski and his wife, but nobody believed him.

Andrzej wanted to regain the respect of the families in the South End, so he pushed himself over the next two days to finish those five tables. Days blended together. Mornings, nights, afternoons. He would pick up an unsanded strip of molding and stare at it for minutes, certain he had just finished the same piece moments or hours before. The only blurs of interaction Andrzej had those days were Tekla's movements floating in and out of the barn. He couldn't remember if seconds or entire afternoons passed between her crossings. Time disintegrated and revolved around the schedule of his body. He fell asleep just before noon. He gulped down his first meal of the day at sunset. Over the first twenty-four hours he took four thirty-minute naps. The second day he somehow forgot to eat. The whole time, Toporski's words kept jabbing him. And that look on his face, festering with such crushing disappointment. He had to find a way to get Dziadzia a table.

Andrzej Kowalczyk's body bolted awake from the pounding at his bedroom door.

Franek threw open the shades and flooded the room with blinding light.

"What time is it?"

"Twenty past three."

Andrzej collapsed back into his pillow, moaning. "Only forty minutes of sleep."

"Where are those tables?"

"I finished all five."

"The ones for *my* order. I don't want those vulgar pieces."

"They are for the people in the neighborhood," Andrzej mumbled, still groggy from sleep.

"I know who they're for. You have three tables left for me, and I need two of them tomorrow morning or you can forget the advance."

That evening Kowalczyk tossed on his boots and coat and shuffled to the barn where Tekla was working. He explained to her how he only had three hours of sleep over the last two days and begged her, pleaded with her to finish the two tables for him. He knew she said she wouldn't help him or Franek, but he needed to sleep and couldn't work anymore.

"Then don't work anymore," she responded and turned back to her carving.

Kowalczyk's body deflated. He dragged himself to his work area and plopped down on a stool to build through the interruption of yawns. Around midnight Andrzej jerked awake from a short nap and hammered with a furious persistence and pushed himself to the early morning hours. Just before sunrise he finished the last of the three tables. If exhaustion hadn't overwhelmed his body, Andrzej would have felt proud of his effort. Instead, he carried his body into the house, past Ty's table in the living room, and collapsed onto his bed. He pulled the covers tightly under his chin and exhaled. His eyes wandered to the ceiling for a moment, then to the wall, then to the window shade, until several hours passed and his body still refused sleep.

Andrzej pried himself out of bed and got a warm mug of milk from the kitchen and returned through the living room. A day didn't go by without Kowalczyk seeing Ty's table. It was a scar reminding him of his own incompetence and mediocrity. He despised that table and its very design. Its craftsmanship. Its splendor. Andrzej wanted to get rid of it. To hide it in the barn or stick it in the boys' bedroom or give it to Stash. Anywhere. Just as long as it wasn't in his sight. But Kowalczyk knew Tekla would never allow that. He couldn't fight with her anymore. Not that he ever fought with her before, he thought. In the past, she had always done what she was told, just as Ty had. But since he had left for Texas, they had defied his every decision. It wasn't their insolence that upset Andrzej the most, but the fact that their choices had been successful. He had been wrong about it all, and they had been right.

The table was there to prove it.

The next night Franek was locking the door to his store for the evening when he was approached by a young man who was the epitome of order. His overcoat was pressed, his boots were somehow polished even through the slop of winter.

"Is this the store with the tables?"

"Yes, it is," Franek said with a smile. "Come right in." He led the young man to the display room and showed him the two tables he had just picked up from Andrzej that morning. "These have already been purchased," he explained, "but I'll be receiving the last table the carpenter ever made by the end of the week. It'll be very expensive."

The man squatted and inspected the piece of furniture. "That won't be a problem."

"How did you hear about my limited collection?" Franek asked.

"Bill Clay told me."

"Do you work with Mr. Clay?"

"No. I'm the supervising lieutenant at the armory."

"Really?" Franek said with a proud gleam. "I served in Cuba."

The lieutenant sprang up and firmly shook Franek's hand. "It's a pleasure to meet you, sir."

"Do you know Major Gansser?"

"Yes, I do."

"I served with him when he was only a sergeant. It was a magnificent war. My name is Kowalczyk. Franek Kowalczyk. He might have told some stories about me from the Battle of Santiago."

"Kowalczyk?" The lieutenant searched his memory. "No, I don't remember him mentioning you, but that name's familiar. Has anyone else in your family served?"

Angry pride flared in Franek's chest. "My older brother Tomaz. But he passed away in Cuba."

"Nope."

Franek tried to restrain the disgust in his voice. "I do have another brother."

———————

Andrzej loaded the cart with tables and yanked it through the thick mud of the South End without anyone offering a hand. The families welcomed Ty's tables, and even Milos Brotzclov showed a sincere grin of appreciation. Andrzej tipped his hat at the fifth house and headed off for his last delivery.

Dziadzia opened the door and stepped onto the porch. Kowalczyk pointed to the cart. Inside was a single table. Toporski turned to Kowalczyk.

"I figured Center Avenue already had enough," Andrzej said.

Toporski slapped him on the back and scampered down the steps. Kowalczyk helped him carry the table into the living room. Dziadzia stepped back, admiring the piece. Every single inch had been carved and crafted by Ty's talented hand.

"Let's celebrate," Toporski insisted.

Kowalczyk's smile faded. "Not tonight."

"Nonsense. The men will be glad to see you."

Andrzej offered more excuses, but Toporski cut him short and led the way to the street. The two men traveled through the slush and hustled into the heat of Pulaski's. Men filled every table and barstool. A few heads turned toward the door, and a hush followed

Kowalczyk as he and Toporski passed. Linkowski and Krymski sneered at him. Zubek was brewing with a new rant. Andrzej felt his chest grow hot as he stepped up to the bar. Stash turned and walked away without a word.

"Two drinks," Toporski ordered.

Kreska and Sawicki approached Kowalczyk and shook his hand. Slowly, other men warmed up to him and offered their condolences. They kidded him about the yellowed bruise around his eye. He was still among friends.

"Kowalczyk," Hryniewicz called out from the card table, "let us deal you in."

Andrzej shook his head. "Not now."

"Come on," Cianek encouraged.

"I do not have money for cards."

"Listen to Kowalczyk," Josef Sczesniak mocked, "with his new wealthy customers, he doesn't have any money."

"That is not why."

"Why then?" Sczesniak challenged. "Why can't you play?"

"Leave him alone, Josef."

"It's fine if he doesn't play."

"I won't leave him alone," Sczesniak shot back. He stood up and approached Kowalczyk. "Is your money too good to waste on us poor Poles?"

Andrzej felt everyone's eyes on him. This was his chance to tell them all about training camp and Texas and the war and everything else, just as he told Tekla he would. But Andrzej Kowalczyk realized he couldn't bring himself to it, not then, not ever. Instead, he told the men to deal him in.

"You don't have to," Toporski said.

"I will play a few hands," Andrzej replied and resigned himself to the fate of the poker table.

Kowalczyk picked up his dealt cards and wasn't surprised to see he only had queen high. He kept that and an eight and threw out three cards. He drew a pair of eights, and his three of a kind prevailed. The hands continued, and Andrzej couldn't believe his luck. Four of the first six pots were his. He should have left then, but he didn't want to take their money so quickly, fearing the men would accuse him of running out on the game. So he kept playing, and the winning hands appeared one after the other: full house, two pair, a flush. Andrzej raked in pot after pot, and some of the men around the table grumbled at Kowalczyk's success. It took another five hours before Andrzej was relieved to have lost the money he had won from the men. That was when he excused himself and walked out into the haze of snowfall. An inescapable void swallowed his stomach as he cursed himself for also losing three-quarters of the money Toporski had paid him, well over thirty-two dollars.

That evening while Tekla and Stanley worked in the barn, Andrzej hid in his bedroom fighting off sleep, trying to pack a small bag. He had decided to leave the next morning. It didn't matter where he went as long as it was far away. If he didn't leave now, he was certain he would become trapped in Bay City— just as he had in Texas—and his discovery by the armory would be inevitable. Besides, he knew he wasn't going to get the advance from Franek. There was no reason to stay. Kowalczyk just wanted to find a place where he could sleep.

The bedroom door pushed open, and Franek poked his head in. "Andrzej, I have a customer for the final table."

Kowalczyk said nothing and stuffed another pair of socks into his bag.

"What are you doing?"

"I am leaving."

"Why?"

"To pay back the loan."

"You said you didn't have enough."

"He needs whatever I can give him," Kowalczyk muttered.

"When are you leaving?"

"Tomorrow morning."

"What about my final order? You have to finish it."

"I will not."

"You won't get that advance I promised you."

"I do not care." Andrzej shoved more clothes into his bag.

His brother grabbed Kowalczyk's arm. "You will give me Ty's last table before you leave."

"There are no more tables," Andrzej said.

"What?"

Kowalczyk pulled away from his brother. "There are no more."

"You promised me ten."

Andrzej said nothing.

"Where is the tenth table?"

Andrzej turned away from his brother and looked inside an empty drawer.

Franek's voice grew harsh. "You sold it, didn't you?"

"No, Franek," his voice dwindled, "there are none."

"Whom did you sell it to?"

Andrzej shook his head.

"Who?" Franek roared.

"Dziadzia."

"Dziadzia Toporski? You're joking. He'll be dead before the end of the year. I'm taking that table."

"He already has it."

"I need that table. I already collected a deposit from the lieutenant."

Andrzej froze. "Who?"

"One of the supervisors at the armory."

"What did you tell him?"

"I told him he would get the last table."

"What did you tell him about me?"

"Nothing."

"I do not believe you. What did he say?"

"Nothing."

Kowalczyk lashed out in vicious desperation. "What did he say?"

Franek paused and held Andrzej's tired eyes. "He said he didn't recognize your name. What should he have said?"

"He must know nothing about me. Nothing!" Kowalczyk crammed everything from the bottom drawer into his bag, certain the military police were on their way to his house at that very moment.

"Fine, I will protect your secret mission," Franek scoffed. "But you will give me that table before you leave."

Kowalczyk slung the bag over his shoulder and rushed past his brother into the hallway.

"Where are you going?" Franek called from behind.

Andrzej sped into the living room, and his brother grabbed him. "Where are you going?"

"I am leaving, Franek." Kowalczyk's voice trembled. "I am leaving."

Franek shoved his face into Andrzej's. "If you won't get Toporski's table back, I'll take this one." He pointed at Ty's table.

Andrzej's eyes widened. He couldn't believe his brother. The suggestion was obscene. A sickness seeped into Kowalczyk's stomach, and he said. "It is yours if you bring me the advance."

Franek drew back, shocked at the response. Then the back door opened. Andrzej glanced over his shoulder, and Tekla walked through the living room and didn't say a word to them.

Kowalczyk looked back at his brother and spoke with a hushed voice. "Well?"

"Fine."

"Meet me in the barn, tomorrow morning, just before sunrise with the money."

Franek nodded. He let himself out of the house and walked through the snow, knowing that he had never intended, before or now, to give Andrzej the advance.

The foreman's men had spent days stuck in the Detroit train station, sleeping in shifts on the wooden benches, asking workers about lumber towns in the center of the state. Standish, Mount Pleasant, Muskegon, Tawas City, and countless others they couldn't remember. There was no way the men could search all of them. They desperately approached travelers exiting the trains arriving from the north, asking if they knew their Polish friend.

Thursday night, just after the 7:26 unloaded, a burly man stopped to buy a newspaper.

"Yeah, I know him," he told them. "Not personally, but he's a legend in those parts."

"Where did you say he lives?"

"Four hours north of here. Bay City. The train'll take you direct."

"How big is this city?"

The traveler shrugged. "Big enough. But people

should know him. Just ask around."

The five supervisors thanked him and headed toward a ticket booth.

The warmth of his bed was hard to resist. For weeks Andrzej Kowalczyk had yearned for a single night of undisturbed sleep, but now when he had the time, he had to force himself to stay awake. He was moving around, sitting up, pacing around his bedroom, slapping his cheeks, but none of this kept him from dozing off. A little after two in the morning, Kowalczyk woke from his latest nap and cursed himself. He yanked himself out of bed, boots already on. He was so tired. He didn't know how he would make it till morning. But he had to get everything ready. Kowalczyk eased his door open and crept down the hallway to Stanley's bedroom. No light glowed from underneath the door. Only faint rhythmic breaths.

Andrzej tiptoed into the living room and stood the table up on one of its short ends. He walked around to the tabletop side and flinched back. A ghastly figure stood behind the glass panes of the table, like the haggard remains of a corpse trapped inside a standing coffin, staring at him. Kowalczyk looked closer. The reflection was his own, but he couldn't believe how sunken his eyes were, how frenzied and withered his face. Was that how Ty looked when he worked so endlessly?

Andrzej crept to the other side of the table, pressed his chest against the bottom shelf, and wrapped his arms around it. It lifted like a dead body, awkward and heavy. Andrzej shuffled out of the living room into the kitchen. Floorboards creaked behind him. Kowalczyk peeked over his shoulder. Nobody was there. He set the table down and kept his eyes fixed on the hallway threshold. The back door wedged open easily, and he moved the table onto the porch.

The porch light was the only glow in the moonless night. Kowalczyk tightened his coat around him and struggled to maneuver the bulky table down the steps. His eyes adjusted to the dark as he walked away from the porch, deeper into the blackness. The icy path through the backyard threatened to throw his feet to the side, but Andrzej steadied his pace to keep his balance. Snow crunched behind him, and he froze. Branches groaned overhead under the weight of ice as he set the table down and looked around. No one was in sight. He turned back to the table, and another crunch, a footstep, came from his left.

"Hello?" Kowalczyk broke the air with a whisper. He peered around the backyard and could only hear the wind rustling through the trees. Andrzej swallowed hard. I am alone, he assured himself. Who would be out this late? He walked forward but couldn't stop envisioning military officials lying in wait, ready to pounce.

Another step. Kowalczyk dropped the table hard and spun around, searching for the figure he heard. He couldn't see anyone. But whoever was there watched his every move. Andrzej hoisted the table and lugged it the rest of the way to the barn.

Inside, the workshop reeked a dry, numbing cold. Andrzej turned on the overhead lights and moved the table to the center of the barn. He retrieved his packed bag from its hiding place in his work area and crammed kindling into the stove. It would be best to wait the couple hours in the barn, Kowalczyk had decided, so he and Franek wouldn't disturb Tekla or Stanley in the morning.

Andrzej yawned as he struck a match and lit the

stove. He had never noticed the quiet in the barn. The winds howled outside, and every area of the workshop creaked and groaned with movement. The table saw loomed in the corner of Andrzej's eye. He tried not to imagine it cutting his son. Ty's countless days and weeks of labor, all ended by one false movement. He shook the vision from his mind and headed for the scrap bin for more wood to fuel the brewing flames.

Kowalczyk froze.

A man darted past the window. Andrzej dashed to the front door and secured the latch. He thought he heard whispering outside. Kowalczyk shut off the lights and hid in the darkness of the corner. The fanged shadows of flames bit spastically, like teeth of a saw blade, into the walls and machinery and lumber inside the barn. Someone leaned against the other side of the door. Andrzej pressed his body against the wall and moved to the back. After every step, he stopped and surveyed the spastic shadows and listened. Something moved overhead, and Kowalczyk ran to the back wall where the axe hung from a nail. He grabbed it and stepped back toward the window, fixing his eyes on it. His feet brushed against something, and he kicked it away. Boards sagged under shifting weight above him, and Andrzej's eyes searched the underbelly of the loft, searched the far corner where a crouching shadow was ready to spring. Kowalczyk's breathing quickened uncontrollably as he neared the window. He swallowed hard and tightened his sweaty hand around the axe handle. He leaned forward and peeked through the window.

A man peered back.

Andrzej screamed and swung the axe at him. The window smashed, and the man disappeared. Andrzej scrambled backwards until a painful jab drove into the small of his back. Kowalczyk twirled around. The extended top of the saw jutted out. He crouched down in the darkness between the saw and Ty's table and watched the window. The man was gone. But Andrzej couldn't take his eyes from the broken glass. The shadows of pulsing flames were dying against the wall, and slowly they dwindled to nothing, leaving Andrzej Kowalczyk in complete darkness.

The barn door shifted behind him, and his shoulders stiffened. Andrzej didn't want to turn and look.

6

Franek arrived the next morning before sunrise just as they had agreed and pounded on the barn door for ten minutes. Then he trudged through the snow to the back porch and peered through the back door window. The kitchen was completely empty. He tapped on the window a few times, and a groggy Tekla walked into the kitchen. Franek tried to think of a good excuse, but she only unlocked the door and headed back toward the bedroom without a word. He stepped inside and shook the snow from his jacket and moved into the living room.

Tekla stood there, fully awake, glaring at him. "Where is it?"

Franek stammered, wringing his hat. "What?"

"What did the two of you do with Ty's table?"

Franek shrugged feebly.

She called out Andrzej's name and headed for his bedroom.

"He owes it to me," Franek called after her.

Tekla whipped open the door and saw the vacant bed and emptied drawers. She shoved her brother-in-law out of the way and raced into the kitchen, searching for her boots. Franek hustled past her and bolted out the door into the clearing, yelling.

That was when Andrzej Kowalczyk's eyes broke from their frozen slumber.

His ears and throat were raw with chills. His hands were swollen and numb. The voice Andrzej heard calling was barely comprehensible. Andrzej sneezed as he pulled his body to its feet. Then he realized it was Franek. Kowalczyk staggered toward the door with the axe still clutched in his hand, then he stopped. Tekla shouted something in the distance, and Kowalczyk moved away from the door.

"Andrzej, I'm here for the table," his brother yelled.

"If you give that to Franek, I'll tell everyone about the letters," Tekla shouted.

"No!" Kowalczyk cried involuntarily. Fists and shouts pounded against the door, as Tekla and Franek battled outside, not over Andrzej, but over Ty's table. For the first time since the night of Ty's death, tears streamed down Kowalczyk's face. He shook his head and muttered to no one, "I can not do it anymore. No more."

"I will tell everyone, everyone!" Tekla threatened.

Kowalczyk turned away and saw Ty's gift.

"If you want that advance, give me that table!" Franek yelled.

Kowalczyk circled the piece of furniture, glaring at it.

"Andrzej!"

He stopped along its short side and lifted the axe above his head. His body teetered, and Kowalczyk tried to steady his shaking hands as tears blinded him.

"Andrzej!"

Kowalczyk brought the blade smashing down. Lumber broke to pieces. A glass pane shattered. Two legs snapped. The axe tore and bit and hacked, pulverizing everything in its path. Splinters and glass shards sprayed continuously until the blade lodged itself into the thick bottom shelf. Andrzej yanked the axe handle, but it wouldn't come free. He dropped to his knees in the dirt and tugged at the axe head. It came loose, and Andrzej flung it to the side. The other half of the table was still intact, angled like a ramp on the ground, and Kowalczyk pulled it toward him. His weeping face appeared in the glass, staring back at him with its vacant eyes. Sobs bellowed from his chest, and Andrzej cocked his arm back. With a spiteful scream, his fist smashed through the solid pane.

And his scream of rage bled into a shriek of pain.

Kowalczyk snatched his hand back and clutched it. Red ooze seeped through his fist, dripping onto the ground. He opened his clenched hand and saw two of his fingers sliced deeply at their bases, hanging in awkward directions. Blood poured from the gashes. Andrzej pressed his injured hand into his armpit and tried to stem the bleeding. He scrambled to his feet and ran to the door. He fell against it and fumbled with the latch. The door swung open, and Kowalczyk collapsed to the icy ground at Franek's and Tekla's feet. Everything grew black.

7

The frigid night wind blasted Stash as he secured his overcoat tightly around him and turned down 31st Street toward his house. The doctors weren't able to save Andrzej's fingers. The ring and pinky fingers on his right hand had to be amputated and the wound cauterized, leaving only burnt stubs. Stash felt no sympathy for his brother-in-law. He would never forgive him.

He walked up his steps, grabbed the keys from his pocket, and unlocked the door.

Drawers from his dresser had been dumped on the floor, torn papers and envelopes strewn across his desk, and whiskey jugs smashed against the wall.

"Janowicz?" a voice whispered behind him.

Stash turned and saw three men in the shadows against the far wall, then a heavy blow struck the back of his neck, knocking him to the floor. Two of the men kicked steel-toed boots into him while Stash tried to protect his head.

"You're lucky we found all the money," the voice snarled.

Blood dripped from Stash's nose and lip. He slid his hands and knees under him. Heels jammed into his lower back and kidneys, and Stash smacked against the floor.

"That's for Mr. Dolton," the voice taunted. "And this is for what you put us through."

A thick board smashed across his shoulders. Adrenaline surged through Stash, and he scanned the room through his swollen eye, searching for the man with the weapon. Stash grabbed the closest leg and yanked it, toppling the assailant to the floor.

The board broke across the back of his head, and the room flashed black, then a blinding white. Stash's body flared with a hot dizziness and the floor spun beneath him. Something instinctual took over, and Stash bolted to his feet. He clutched the collar of the man in front of him and blindly unleashed a series of punches to the man's face. All the time the board cracked against his back.

Stash spit warm blood and slid behind the man he held. He tightened an arm around his throat and grabbed him by his hair. In one motion, Stash snapped the man's neck, and the entire body sagged in his arms.

"That's not Janowicz!" the voice yelled out as Stash threw the dead body to the side.

He picked up the chair beside him and brandished it toward the men scrambling for the door. Stash took a step forward and his legs wobbled beneath him. The room spiraled, and he slammed the chair down to brace himself. He leaned against it and pressed his hand across the bleeding gash in his head. Stash tried to ease himself onto the chair, but his strength failed, and he missed the seat, falling to the floor. His body twitched before losing consciousness.

Part Four

1

On November 11, 1918, red, white, and blue festivities swept the country as everyone celebrated the end of the Great War. Ticker tape parades showered big city streets across the nation. Fireworks burst with applause and excitement as onlookers blew whistles and waved flags. Prohibited kegs of beer rolled out of hiding spots, and every child and adult drank to the American troops and the country they honored. Families and friends shared hugs and tears as they waited for their loved ones to come home.

Bay City's rejoicing was undercut by death. Days before the end of the War, a deadly influenza epidemic struck the area. Over its duration the illness killed scores of people and left more than 1,400 sick. The casualties were mostly children and the elderly, but young men and women didn't escape the debilitating symptoms. Many of those who cheered the American soldiers were bedridden with high fevers, wearing surgical masks to protect those around them. As the cases escalated, schools and public buildings were closed, and the countless horse-drawn carriages lined up around Samaritan Hospital offered little encouragement to the sick.

The devastation hit every neighborhood in Bay City just as severely as the South End. Marija Zietek, Jonah Kosinski, Herb Gruszka, and Abe Krupa died in those first days and never had a chance to see the victory in Europe. Dziadzia Toporski held Busia's hand and just before she passed away he heard her repeat to him, in a whisper of Polish, the same loving promise they had exchanged fifty-two years ago as their ship set sail for America.

The Kowalczyks were unaffected by the epidemic, but they had enough suffering to bear. Andrzej had packed himself into a silent chair in the far corner of the living room. His days passed gazing out the window, staring at nothing. For hours at a time he didn't move. He was as good as dead.

The attack at Stash's house terrified the South End and perplexed the local police. Everyone knew Stash had no enemies, and the stranger's dead body offered few clues for the investigators. None of the neighbors had any information, other than Mrs. Rozanski who saw four figures fleeing down the street after she heard the yells that night. Andrzej Kowalczyk suspected the truth but didn't say a word to anyone.

Tekla tried to put the events of that day and night out of her mind, but there were plenty of afternoons and evenings when the memories were too much, and the tears flowed. She had cleaned up the bits of the fragmented table and preserved the two legs and side that were still intact and hung them from a nail above her carving bench. She found relief carvings pieces, and her memories of Ty and his table made things more bearable. And once Stash's broken collarbone and ribs healed, they would fill the rest of the original orders.

Days passed before Andrzej Kowalczyk was able to look over his shoulder at the vacancy that had been the table. He knew Tekla left the space there to mock him. He had destroyed that scar, but now his deformed hand, with its burnt skin and phantom itches, would haunt him for as long as he lived. He considered cutting away the charred flesh to rid himself of it. But that would only leave a new scar that would have to be cut away, and that would leave another, and another, and another. . . .

The next afternoon Stanley stuck his head in the living room and announced a visitor.

"Good day, Kowalczyk," Toporski said as he stepped into the threshold. A figure clad in a long overcoat and a wide-brimmed hat stood behind him.

Andrzej stood up and stuffed his hand into the pocket of his sweater.

Toporski looked over his shoulder. "I brought Ignasiu like you asked."

Kowalczyk stepped forward to shake hands, but stopped. Ignasiu peeked out from his upturned collar at Andrzej's hand. Ignasiu held Andrzej's eyes for a moment. Kowalczyk offered a weak smile and stuffed his fist back into his pocket and extended his left hand. Ignasiu took off his hat and revealed his boyish face. Scabs and gouges from shrapnel marred its left side. Andrzej swallowed hard. He felt embarrassed in his presence. Ignasiu unbuttoned his overcoat and struggled to remove it. The left sleeve of his shirt was pinned to the shoulder. His arm was missing from below the elbow.

Andrzej couldn't take his eyes from the young man's pinned sleeve. Ignasiu offered his right hand, and Kowalczyk pulled his scarred hand from its hiding spot. The two men shook.

"Have a seat, Ignasiu," Kowalczyk said. "Toporski?"

Dziadzia shook his head. "No, thank you. I have to finish the route. Ignasiu, you'll be fine getting home?"

"Yes, sir."

Toporski left the room. The two men sat in silence,

staring off in different directions. Andrzej had thought it would be good to finally meet Ignasiu, but now he wanted to flee the room. He fidgeted in his chair and shifted his eyes toward the young man, trying to look at his missing arm. Ignasiu caught him staring, and Kowalczyk glanced away, trying to pretend he wasn't looking. He gazed down at his own charred nubs.

"Dziadzia says you are a big Tigers fan," Andrzej finally said.

Ignasiu shrugged. "Yes, sir."

"Cobb had a fabulous season. If only the rest of the team was any good."

Ignasiu nodded politely. "I didn't hear many games over there."

"Oh." Kowalczyk felt a heat in his face. He stared off at the floor.

"Mr. Kowalczyk, I wanted to talk—" Ignasiu's voice broke, his hand tapping his knee. He inhaled and let out a slow breath. "I don't know where to begin."

"We do not have to," Andrzej offered.

"No, please, I need to." Ignasiu paused, staring at his knee. "We didn't mean to do what we did, Mr. Kowalczyk. When me and Mitch Brozka and Pete Mroczek and Charlie and his kid brother left Texas, we wanted to show Europe how great Americans were. But once you get there, it's nothing but bombs and gunfire and blood and that stench." His fingers tightened around his knee. "Pete was the first to go. I mean, they tell you in church death is this glorious moment filled with peace and reflection. But it's not. He stepped on a landmine that morning. He didn't even know what happened. He was just gone.

"A couple weeks later we lost Mitch crawling out of the trench. Enemy fire hit him in the gut, and he fell back in. I was by him and he grabbed my hand. He looked me in the eyes and said, 'Ignasiu, you get home and talk to Mr. Kowalczyk.'" The young man swallowed hard, glancing at Andrzej for the first time. "Then his eyes started to fade. But he kept talking, saying how God was punishing us, all of us, for what we'd done. He said it was up to me to be the messenger. He squeezed my hand and prayed to God right then and there to keep me alive. Just so I could come home and talk to you. Then he died. Right there in the stench. With those vacant eyes on me.

"I thought what he said was just the craziness of death, but four days later, Charlie took an easy bullet in the calf. You know, the kind of wounds soldiers hope for, beg for, because it's their ticket home. Everyone congratulated him, and they hauled him to the med tent. But that's the most deadly place in the whole damn war. The filth and disease there. The rot ate into his leg and kept on eating. He was dead in three days. When his kid brother found out, he rushed into battle the next day, just looking to die."

Ignasiu paused. A smile eased across his lips as a tear dripped down his cheek. "God's got a funny sense of humor," his voice cracked. "That's why He took my arm and sent me home just like Mitch asked. We were just kids, Mr. Kowalczyk, we didn't know. We didn't know."

Andrzej felt his eyes well up. He looked to the side and coughed a few times. "Ignasiu, I—" He cleared his throat again. "Toporski said you wanted to talk to someone about Europe. To someone who had the same type of experiences you had." Andrzej paused, trying to look the young man in the eye. He couldn't. "I did not have those same experiences." He held up his hand. "I lost these here in an accident. And all those stories about me being a hero," his throat tightened, "they are not true. I am sorry."

Ignasiu laughed one of those laughs a person uses to

hold back the flood of tears. "I know you didn't serve, Mr. Kowalczyk. That's what I wanted to talk to you about."

Andrzej looked up, confused. "I do not understand, Ignasiu. How do you know?"

"That was all you ever talked about in Texas, being a hero. You wanted to be a hero." The quivering smile melted from the young man's face. "God took my arm, Mr. Kowalczyk, the same arm I used to write that letter I sent home, letters we all sent home, saying you were on a secret mission. We did it for a good laugh, a joke, that's all." His voice trembled. "And God punished us for our lies. He punished all of us for our lies."

Ignasiu buried his head into his hand and cried loud, deep sobs.

———————

After Ignasiu left, Andrzej stepped into the kitchen and slid his feet into his boots.

Stanley hustled in through the back door from his paper route and stopped when he saw his father. He walked past him.

"Stanley," Andrzej called.

His son turned around.

"Do me a favor," he said. "I know she will not care, but tell your mother I have told people the truth. I have told them the truth." Andrzej stood up and gave his son a long embrace.

Stanley stepped back from his father, confused. "All right."

Andrzej grabbed his overcoat and walked toward the door.

"Where are you going?" Stanley asked.

"I need to see Ty."

By the time Andrzej hiked the mile to St. Stanislaus Cemetery and trudged through the deep snow to the grave, the frost had gnawed the edges of his ears and hands. He bundled the warmth of his coat around him and rubbed his hands together. Only the top of the snow-covered grave peeked out. Kowalczyk reached down with his deformed hand and scooped away the icy crust of snow. He knelt down and dug deeper and deeper until the entire face of the grave was cleared. He blew into the hot throbbing of his hands and looked at the ice caked on the surface of the stone. With the two fingers of his deformed hand, Kowalczyk chiseled into the snow-packed letters and kept etching away until long after his flesh was raw and frostbitten. Tears streamed down his face as he carved every letter clean on his son's tomb. He sat back on his heels and let the words on the grave-stone burn into his mind.

Stanley sprinted out of the house to join his mother in the barn when he saw three men walking up the drive.

"Where's your father?"

Stanley stepped back. "He went to see Ty."

Snow fell as light drained from the sky. Kowalczyk saw the men approaching in the distance. He stood up and tried to rub feeling back into his scarred hand. One man split away from the two uniformed officers and advanced toward him.

"Andrzej, what the hell is going on here?" Franek

demanded. "The lieutenant ordered me from my store and marched me here without telling me a thing."

"I asked them to bring you."

"I don't understand."

"The lieutenant is going to take me away and—"

"What do you mean?"

"Let me explain, Franek."

His brother snorted and folded his arms across his chest.

Andrzej's eyes drifted down to the snow. "I do not know when I will return, Franek, or if I will return at all. Soon, you will hear stories about me. Stories about me not really being on a secret mission, or going to Europe, or even fighting in the war. Or stories about me picking crops in Texas, or stealing money while I was there, or how those men who attacked Stash were really looking for me."

Andrzej looked up from his footmarks in the snow and saw the confusion in Franek's face.

"But I needed to tell you this myself," Kowalczyk continued, "before you heard it from anyone else." He stared directly into his brother's eyes. "Because all of those stories are lies. Lies to protect the other soldiers on the secret mission. The army is afraid of another attack, just like the one at Stash's. So they are moving me to a secret place somewhere in the country. That is all I can tell you, Franek, but I wanted one person to know the truth about me. Promise me you will not tell anyone else."

Franek didn't know what to say, so he nodded.

"I have to go." And with that Andrzej Kowalczyk stuffed his deformed hand into his pocket and walked over to the officers, wondering if his brother had believed a word he said.

THE END

Acknowledgments

I would like to thank the people who helped make this novel what it is. Foremost, my editor, Amy Braden, for her advice and persistency thoughout the evolution of this creative work. Scott Baier, Dara Hanke, and Todd Noonan for their suggestions on the finer points. And everyone who contributed resources and their own stories of Bay City's history, especially Ellie Majchrzak, Janet Wrobel, and Stan Wiechec.

About the author

Matthew Waynee is a writer and filmmaker living in Los Angeles. He currently teaches writing at the University of Southern California.

Galt Art House

Check out other titles at
www.galtarthouse.com